"You didn't have to bundle me up like that, you know." Rose gave a little cough. *"I've not been well."*

"So I've been told." Hassan didn't sound convinced by her act. "You seem to be having a good time, though. Personally, I wouldn't have thought that cocktail parties, receptions and tours of the city were good for you—"

"Oh, I *see*! You're doing me a *kindness*. You've abducted me so that I shouldn't overexert myself."

"I do my best." He ignored her snort of disbelief. "You came to my country for a holiday. A little romance, perhaps?"

Oh, good grief! If he was into fulfilling holiday fantasies, she was in big trouble....

Born and raised in Berkshire, **Liz Fielding** started writing at the age of twelve, when she won a hymn-writing competition at her convent school. After a gap of more years than she is prepared to admit to, during which she worked as a secretary in Africa and the Middle East, got married and had two children, she was finally able to realize her ambition and turn to full-time writing in 1992.

She now lives with her husband, John, in west Wales, surrounded by mystical countryside and romantic, crumbling castles, content to leave the traveling to her grown-up children and keeping in touch with the rest of the world via the Internet.

Praise for *His Desert Rose* from *Romantic Times Magazine*:

"Talented storyteller Liz Fielding...
utilizes emotional scenes, a powerful internal conflict
and an exotic desert setting and culture to bring together
two dynamic characters."

Books by Liz Fielding

HARLEQUIN ROMANCE®
3570—AND MOTHER MAKES THREE

HIS DESERT ROSE
Liz Fielding

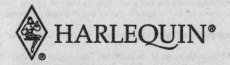

HARLEQUIN®

TORONTO • NEW YORK • LONDON
AMSTERDAM • PARIS • SYDNEY • HAMBURG
STOCKHOLM • ATHENS • TOKYO • MILAN • MADRID
PRAGUE • WARSAW • BUDAPEST • AUCKLAND

ISBN 0-373-03618-3

HIS DESERT ROSE

First North American Publication 2000.

Copyright © 2000 by Liz Fielding.

CHAPTER ONE

'THERE was a journalist on the plane, Partridge.' Prince Hassan al Rashid joined his aide in the rear of the limousine. 'Rose Fenton. She's a foreign correspondent for one of the television news networks. Find out what she's doing here.'

'There's no mystery about it, Excellency. She's convalescing from pneumonia. That's all.' Hassan favoured the man with a look that doubted his sanity. But then Partridge was young, British and unbelievably innocent when it came to politics, whereas he had learned the game at his grandfather's knee and suspected it would be very far from 'all'. 'She's Tim Fenton's sister,' Partridge added helpfully. As if that explained everything. 'He's the new Chief Veterinary Officer,' he continued, when he realised it didn't. 'He thought a little sun would help with his sister's recuperation.'

'Did he?' How convenient. 'And since when did being related to the CVO entitle anyone, let alone a journalist, to a seat on Abdullah's private jet?'

'I believe that His Highness thought Miss Fenton would appreciate the extra comfort, after being so ill. He's apparently a great admirer...' Hassan's response was a dismissive wave of the hand, but Partridge stuck to his guns. 'And since you were coming home anyway—'

'I only learned about the flight when I asked the em-

bassy to organise my own travel arrangements. We both
know that Abdullah wouldn't fly a kite for my convenience. As for offering his personal flying palace…'

'I think His Highness is fully aware of your opinion
of his extravagance.'

'Yes, well, even the Queen of England flies on a
commercial airliner these days.'

'His Highness doesn't want the Queen of England to
write a flattering piece about him for one of the major
news magazines.'

Not that innocent, then. 'Thank you, Partridge.'
Hassan briefly acknowledged his aide's unusually wry
touch of humour. 'I was sure you would get to the point
eventually.'

Unfortunately it was not something to laugh about.
Rose Fenton would doubtless be fêted and flattered as
part of the Regent's charm offensive while Faisal, the
youthful Emir, was conveniently out of the country
studying American business methods and showing no
great eagerness to return home. His own return, Hassan
thought grimly, had been precipitated by a friendly
whisper that Abdullah was on the point of turning his
Regency into something more permanent.

'Is she aware what's expected of her?' he asked.

'I shouldn't think so.'

Hassan wasn't convinced. 'What about her brother?
Have you met him?'

'At the sports club,' he said. 'On the social circuit.
Tim Fenton's good company. He asked for leave to go
home when his sister was taken ill and before he knew
what was happening His Highness had issued a personal
invitation for her to visit Ras al Hajar to convalesce.'

'And when my cousin makes up his mind to something, it's a foolish man who argues.' And why would Rose Fenton argue? Abdullah kept foreign journalists out of Ras al Hajar as a matter of policy. And there weren't any local ones. This must have seemed like a gift.

'I don't think you need worry, sir. Miss Fenton's reputation as a journalist is formidable. If your cousin is looking for some flattering publicity I'd say he's chosen the wrong woman.'

'Maybe. Tell me, does Tim Fenton like his job here?'

Partridge's silence was all the reply he required. Rose Fenton wouldn't need to have it spelt out for her in words of one syllable either; she was far too clever for that. And Abdullah would make it easy for her. He'd tell the woman what a great job he was doing, and to prove it he'd whisk her in air-conditioned luxury from the new medical centre to the new shopping mall, via the new sports facilities. Progress in stainless steel and reinforced concrete.

He'd keep her sufficiently busy so that she wouldn't have time to go looking for anything that might give her other ideas. Even if she had a mind to. After all, a one-to-one interview with the media-shy Regent would be a serious scoop for any journalist, no matter how formidable her reputation.

Hassan wasn't as enamoured of journalists as his aide, even when they came packaged like the lovely Rose Fenton.

He changed tack. 'Tell me, Partridge, since you're so well informed, what entertainments has my cousin arranged to keep the lady amused while she's here? I imagine he *does* have plans to keep her amused?' The idea was distasteful, but he knew that if Abdullah admired the lady it was for her lovely face and fiery red hair rather than her journalistic skills. Partridge's quick flush demonstrated exactly the effect Miss Fenton produced on susceptible males. 'Well?'

'There have been some activities arranged,' he confirmed. 'A dhow trip along the coast, a feast somewhere in the desert, a tour of the city...'

'She appears to be getting the full red carpet treatment.' Although he suspected her feet wouldn't touch the ground long enough for her to feel it. 'Anything else?'

'Well, there's a cocktail party at the British Embassy, of course...' Then he hesitated.

'Why do I have the feeling that you're saving the best until last?'

'His Highness is hosting a reception at the palace in her honour.'

'Practically a State visit, then,' he said, all his worst fears confirmed. 'But rather an exhausting schedule for a woman convalescing from pneumonia, wouldn't you say?'

'She *has* been ill, Excellency. She collapsed reporting to camera from somewhere in Eastern Europe. I saw it happen. She just pitched forward...for a moment I thought she'd been shot by a sniper. How did she look?' He asked anxiously, 'You did see her on the plane?'

'Only briefly. She looked...'

Hassan paused briefly to consider exactly how Rose Fenton had looked. A little flushed, perhaps. The ruffled collar of her white blouse had provided a frame for a face that was a little thinner than the last time he'd seen her on a satellite news broadcast. Maybe that was why her dark eyes had seemed so large.

Dressed for warmth against the raw chill of the weather, she'd been wearing a scarlet sweater that should have clashed horribly with her red hair, but hadn't. On the contrary; the effect had been riveting.

She'd looked up from a book she was holding and met his glance with frank curiosity; it had been a confident look that avoided being in any way flirtatious but had still managed to convey the suggestion that she'd welcome his company to while away the tedious hours in the air.

Honesty forced him to concede that he'd been tempted, his own curiosity thoroughly roused by her presence on his cousin's private jet. And he was not impervious to the pleasure of a beautiful woman's company to help pass the time.

At one point he'd got as far as summoning the steward to invite her forward. In the few seconds it had taken the man to respond, common sense had reasserted itself.

Mixing with journalists was not a good idea. A man just never knew what they'd print next. Or rather he did know. Too late, he'd learned that it was far easier to gain a reputation than lose it, especially if the reputation suited a certain highly placed individual.

And Abdullah would certainly hear about any conversation they'd shared the minute the wheels touched down. Being seen with him would do her no good at all in palace circles.

She'd be safer sticking to her book, no matter how

unexpected her choice. Fantasy was always less dangerous than the real thing.

He realised that Partridge was still waiting for his answer. 'She looked well enough,' he said irritably.

Rose Fenton stopped to catch her breath as she stepped out of the chill of the air-conditioned arrival hall of the airport and into the midday heat of Ras al Hajar.

Despite the brave show of daffodils in the parks, London hadn't quite made spring, and Rose had been bundled up in thermal underwear and a heavy sweater by her unusually anxious mother.

'Are you all right, Rose? You must be tired from the journey.'

'Don't fuss, Tim.' Her brother's anxious query made him sound exactly like their mother and she wasn't used to being fussed over. It made her realise just how sick she'd been. She peeled off the sweater. 'I'm not an invalid, just hot,' she snapped, her irritability a sure indication that she wasn't feeling quite as lively as she would have everyone believe. She'd been very bad-tempered the week before she collapsed with pneumonia, but Tim's obvious concern made her instantly contrite. 'Oh, heck, I'm sorry. It's just that for the last month Mum's been treating me like some nineteenth-century heroine about to expire from consumption.' Her smile took on a slightly mischievous slant as she hooked her arm through his. 'I thought I'd escaped the leash.'

'Yes, well, I have to admit you don't look quite as bad as I'd expected from the way she's been fretting,' he retaliated, easily slipping into the old habit of brotherly teasing, not in the least in awe of her distinguished reputation as a foreign correspondent. 'I was beginning to wonder if I should rent a bath-chair for your visit.'

'That really won't be necessary.'

'Just a walking stick, then?'

'Only if you want me to beat you with it.'

'You're definitely on the mend,' he said, laughing.

'I had two choices: recover quickly, or die of boredom. Mum wouldn't let me read anything more taxing than a three-year-old magazine,' she told him as he ushered her in the direction of a dusty dark green Range Rover. 'And when she discovered I was watching the news, she threatened to confiscate my TV.'

'You're exaggerating, Rose.'

'As if I would!' Then she relented. 'Well, maybe. Just a bit.' And she grinned. 'But I'm not tired, really. Travelling in the Emir's private jet had about as much in common with flying economy as a bicycle has with a Rolls Royce.' She grinned. 'It's flying, Tim, but not as we know it.' She breathed in the warm desert air. 'This is what I need. Let me get out of these thermals,' she said, 'and you won't be able to stop me.'

'I warn you, I'm under strict orders to keep you from doing anything too physical.'

'Spoilsport. I was banking on being whisked away on a fiery black stallion by some hawk-nosed desert prince,' she teased, but, since her brother looked less than impressed with that idea, she squeezed his arm reassuringly. 'Just kidding. Gordon gave me a copy of *The Sheik* to read on the plane.' Her news editor's idea of a joke, no doubt. He had an odd sense of humour. Or maybe it had been an excuse to hand over the bookshop carrier that contained all the information he'd been able to dig up on the situation in Ras al Hajar right under her mother's watchful eyes. She patted the bag slung over her shoulder. 'I'm not sure whether it was meant as inspiration or warning.'

'You mean you actually read it?'

'It's a classic of women's fiction,' she protested.

'Well, I hope you took it as a warning. I've had my instructions from Ma and, believe me, horse riding of any description is definitely off the agenda. You're allowed to lie in the shade by the pool with a little light reading in the morning, but only if you promise not to go in the water—'

'I've had weeks of this, Tim. I am not promising anything.'

'Only if you promise not to go in the water,' he repeated, with a broad grin, 'and have a little nap in the afternoon.' Then, more gently, 'You gave us all a terrible fright, you know, collapsing in the middle of the evening news.'

'Very bad form,' she agreed briskly. 'I'm supposed to report the news, not make it...' Her voice trailed off as she watched a long black limousine, windows darkened, speed away from the airport.

The car's occupant was undoubtedly the reason for the flight of the Emir's private jet on which her brother had managed to hitch her a ride. Wearing an immaculately tailored dark suit, a discreetly striped shirt and a silk tie, he could have been the chairman of any large public company boarding his private plane moments before take-off. But he wasn't.

Their gazes had met and mutual recognition had been

instant before the door to her cabin had been hurriedly shut by an apologetic stewardess more used to travelling princesses than nosy journalists.

Which had been a pity. Prince Hassan al Rashid came very high on her must-meet list. Amongst the pile of news clippings, the photograph of the hawkish face with piercing grey eyes had been the only one that had caught her attention and held it. If Rose had been seriously seeking her own personal fantasy adventure with a sheikh, on a horse of any colour, he would have fulfilled the role admirably.

Prince Hassan had paused as he'd entered the aircraft, and in the moment before the door was shut those grey eyes had fixed her with a look that had brought a flush of colour to her cheeks and made her want to tug her calf-length skirt closer to her ankles. It was a look that had left her feeling entirely female, entirely vulnerable in a way that for a twenty-eight-year-old journalist was almost embarrassing.

A twenty-eight-year-old journalist, with one marriage, one war and half a dozen in-depth interviews with prime ministers and presidents behind her.

But she was quite capable of recognising a seriously dangerous man when she saw one, and his photograph, a posed, expressionless, formal portrait, hadn't even come close to the real thing.

What, if any, impression she had made upon him was impossible to tell. In the few moments before the door had been closed discreetly between them, his expression had given nothing away.

It was her first taste of purdah and, despite the fact that she'd been treated throughout the flight like a princess, she didn't much like it. She knew that, by his own standards, Prince Hassan was showing her far more respect by ignoring her presence than if he had joined her, but as a journalist she could scarcely help being disappointed. It was her disappointment as a woman that disturbed her more.

Besides, such respect seemed strangely at odds with his reputation as a playboy prince whose wealth, according to gossip, was pumped straight from his country's oil wells to the wrists and necks of beautiful women, and the world's most exclusive gaming tables.

But at home in Ras al Hajar he apparently chose to at least nod to convention. When he had disembarked before her, to be greeted by the officials lined up on the tarmac, he had dispensed with the expensive Italian tailoring and was wearing the trappings of a desert prince. A black prince.

The breeze had tugged impatiently at the gossamer-thin camel hair cloak thrown over his black robes, at the black *keffiyeh* held in place by a simple, unadorned camel halter. And she had sensed his own impatience with the ceremonial honour paid him as each man stepped forward to take his hands and bow deeply over them.

Tim saw her glance drawn to the limousine as the morning sun flashed from the darkened windows. 'Prince Hassan,' he murmured.

'Prince who?' she asked, feigning ignorance. She had long since learned that people told her far more that way.

But Tim did not leap in with the local gossip as she

had hoped. 'No one for you to get worked up about, Rose. He's only the local playboy.'

'Really? From all the bowing and scraping when he got off the plane, I thought he must be next in line to King around here.'

'He's not next in line to anything.' Tim shrugged. 'Hassan warrants all that "bowing and scraping", as you so eloquently put it, because his father took a bullet meant for the old Emir. Several bullets, in fact.'

'Oh?' Act dumb, Rosie, just act dumb. 'He was shot?'

Tim's disbelieving glance warned her that she might have gone a bit over the top, but he indulged her curiosity. 'Yes, he was shot, and his reward for a bullet in the shoulder and a smashed leg was the hand of the old Emir's favourite daughter and a life of ease. Not that he lived long enough to enjoy it.'

'He didn't survive the attack, then?'

'He made a pretty fair recovery, by all accounts, but he was killed in a car accident a few months after the wedding.'

'How terrible.' Then, '*Was* it an accident?'

Her brother's mouth straightened in a knowing grin. 'Quick for a girl, aren't you?' Then he shrugged. 'Your guess is as good as mine and that's all anyone can do— guess.'

'Well, he lived long enough to father a son,' she said, regret stirring at deeply buried memories. 'That's as close to immortality as any of us ever gets.'

'Rose,' Tim prompted gently.

She responded with a distracted, 'Mmm,' as she continued to watch the limousine speed away from the airport. It might be her job to be interested in anyone who was so close to the throne yet could never aspire to it, but something else was prompting her curiosity about the man behind those grey eyes.

She'd met men who could command the most undisciplined rabble with no more than a look from eyes like that. It wasn't the colour that mattered, it was the strength, the conviction behind them. His weren't the eyes of a playboy. And if he was pretending? The thought strayed into her head and stirred the down on the nape of her neck.

Then, realising that Tim was still patiently holding the door for her, she smiled. 'So, I like a good human interest story. Tell me about him. His father must have been dead before he was born.'

'He was. Perhaps that's why Hassan was so indulged by the old man. He was raised as a favourite.' Tim glanced back at the limousine, disappearing at speed in the direction of the open desert. 'Too much money, too little to do; it was bound to lead to trouble.'

'What kind of trouble?'

He shrugged. 'Women, gambling... But what can you expect? A man has to do something, and despite the title he's effectively barred from palace politics.'

'Oh? Why's that?' She was too quick with the question and Tim suddenly realised that he was being pumped for information.

'Leave it, Rose,' he said firmly. 'You're here for rest and recuperation, not to ferret out a non-existent story.'

'But if you don't tell me why he can't get involved in politics I'll just worry about it,' she said, quite reasonably, as Tim helped her up into the air-conditioned comfort of the four-wheel drive. 'I just won't be able to help myself.'

'Try. Very hard,' he suggested. 'This isn't a democracy and nosy journalists are not welcome.'

'I'm not nosy,' she said, with a grin. 'Just interested.' Prince Hassan interested her a lot. Men with eyes like that didn't waste time playing...not without good reason.

'And I'm Charley's Aunt. You're here as Prince Abdullah's guest, Rosie. Break the rules and you'll be on the first flight out of here. And so will I, so drop it. Please.'

It was years since Tim had called her Rosie, and she suspected that this was his way of reminding her that, despite the fact that she was a well-known and respected journalist, she was still his little sister. And this was his territory. So she shrugged and let the subject drop. For now. Besides, she knew, or suspected she knew, the answer to her question. Hassan's father might have been a hero, but he'd been a foreigner, a Scot who'd been drawn to the desert. She had the press cuttings to prove it.

But it wouldn't do to let Tim know that. 'Sorry, it's just force of habit. And boredom.'

'Then we'll have to make sure that you don't get bored. I've arranged a small party to introduce you to some people, and Prince Abdullah has pulled out all the stops to make sure you have a good time.'

Rose allowed Tim to run on about the receptions and parties lined up and waiting for her pleasure, not pushing the subject she was most interested in. After all, receptions and parties were the places to hear all the latest gossip and, with luck, meet the local playboy.

'What was that about a reception at the palace?' she asked, tuned in for the important words even while her brain was thinking about something else.

'Only if you feel up to it,' he added. He glanced across at her and pulled a little face. 'I should warn you that the ride in Abdullah's private plane might have strings attached. He's not above trying to charm you into recording a flattering interview with him.'

'Well, he's out of luck,' she said, mentally scratching the interview with Abdullah, number two on her Ras al Hajar must-do list. A pity, but it would give her more time to concentrate on Prince Hassan. After all, she was on holiday and entitled to a treat. 'I'm here to relax.'

'Since when did relaxation get in the way of work? I can't see you turning down an exclusive interview with the ruler of a strategically important and oil-rich country, no matter how sick you've been.'

'Regent,' she reminded him, abandoning all pretence. 'Isn't the young Emir due back from America soon? Or could it be that now he's had a taste of life at the top, Prince Abdullah is reluctant to step down? I mean, once you've been King anything else has to be something of an anticlimax. Doesn't it?' Tim frowned, his glance suddenly anxious. She grinned and put a reassuring hand on his arm. 'I'll just stick to lying quietly by the pool with a little light reading, shall I? Relaxing.'

He swallowed. 'Perhaps that would be best. I'll tell His Highness that you're too weak for partying just yet.'

'Don't you dare! Tell him... Tell him, I'm just to weak to work.'

Hassan remained deep in thought for a long time after the car had come to a halt. 'You'll have to go to the States, Partridge. It's time Faisal was home.'

'But Excellency—'

'I know, I know.' He waved impatiently. 'He's enjoying the freedom and he won't want to come, but he can't put it off any longer.'

'He'd take it better from you, sir.'

'Maybe, but the fact that I feel unable to leave the country will ram home the message more effectively than anything either of us can say.'

'What do you want me to say?'

'Tell him...tell him if he wants to keep his country, it's time to come home before Abdullah takes it from him. I can't put it plainer than that.'

He climbed from the limousine and strode towards the huge carved doors of the coastal watch-tower he had made his home, his feet ringing on the stone slabs of the courtyard.

'And Miss Fenton?' Partridge asked, his pace slower as he leaned heavily on his walking stick.

Hassan paused at the entrance to his private apartments. 'You can safely leave Miss Fenton to me,' he said sharply.

Partridge paled, swinging round in front of him and forcing him to a halt. 'Sir, you won't forget she's been ill—'

'I won't forget that she's a journalist.' Hassan's face darkened as he saw the anxiety in the man's face. Well,

well. Lucky Rose Fenton. Needed by a fabulously rich and totally powerful older man for her ability to make him look good, desired by a young and foolish one with nothing in his head but romantic nonsense. All in one day. How many women could start a holiday with that kind of advantage?

It occurred to him that Rose Fenton, blessed with both brains and beauty, probably started every holiday with that kind of advantage.

'What are you planning to do, sir?'

'Do?' He wasn't used to having his intentions questioned.

Partridge might be nervous, but he wasn't cowed. 'With Miss Fenton.'

Hassan gave a short laugh. 'What do you *think* I'm going to do with her, man?' The image of the book she had been holding swept into his mind. 'Abduct her and carry her off into the desert like some old-time bandit?'

Partridge immediately flushed. 'N-no.'

'You don't sound very certain,' he pressed. 'It's what my grandfather would have done.'

'Your grandfather lived in a different age, sir,' Partridge said. 'I'll go and pack.'

Hassan watched him go. The young man had guts, and he admired him for the way he coped with disability and pain, but he wouldn't put up with dissent from anyone. He'd do whatever he had to.

Thirty minutes later he handed Partridge the letter he had written to his young half-brother and walked with him to the Jeep that would take him down to the jetty. The courtyard was full of horsemen with hawks at their wrists, long-legged silky-coated Salukis at their heels.

Partridge's eyes narrowed. 'You're going hunting? Now?'

'I need to heat the London damp out of my bones and get some good, clean desert air in my lungs.' And it occurred to him that if Abdullah was planning a quiet coup, it might be wise to take himself to his desert camp where his presence would be less noticeable. 'I'll speak to you tomorrow.'

'This is it.'

'It's beautiful, Tim.' The villa was out of the town, set on the hillside overlooking the wild and rugged coast near the royal stables. Tim's title might give him control of the country's veterinary services, but his main concern was the Regent's stud. Below them was a palm grove and around the house there were oleanders in flower, bright birds... 'I expected desert...sand dunes...'

'Hollywood has a lot to answer for.' The door opened at their approach and Tim's servant bowed as Rose crossed the threshold. 'Rose, this is Khalil. He cooks, cleans and looks after the place so I can concentrate on work.' The young man returned her smile shyly.

'Good grief, Tim,' Rose said, once she'd admired everything, from the exquisite rugs laid over polished hardwood floors to the small swimming pool in the discreetly walled garden beyond the French windows. 'It's a bit different from that scruffy little house you had in Newmarket.'

'If you think this is luxury, just wait until you see the stables. The horses have a much larger swimming pool than me and I have a fully equipped hospital, anything I ask for—'

'Okay, okay!' She grinned at his enthusiasm. 'You can give me the grand tour later, but right now I could do with a shower.' She lifted her hair from her neck. 'And I need to change into some lighter clothes.'

'What? Oh, sorry. Look, why don't you make yourself at home, have a rest, something to eat? Your room is through here.' He shepherded her through to a large suite. 'There's plenty of time to see everything.'

She stopped in the doorway, but it wasn't the splendour of her room that surprised her. It was the fact that every available surface was obscured by baskets full of roses. 'Where on earth did all these come from?'

'Wherever roses are grown at this time of year.' Tim shrugged, obviously embarrassed by the excess. 'I should have thought you were used to it by now. I don't suppose anyone ever sends you lilies, or daisies or chrysanthemums. Do they?'

'Rarely,' she admitted, looking for a card, but finding none. 'But they usually come in dozens. These appear to have been ordered by the gross.'

'Yes, well, Prince Abdullah sent them over this morning so that you'd feel at home.'

'He thinks I live in a florist's shop?'

Tim pulled a face. 'They do everything on a grander scale here.' He glanced anxiously at his watch. 'Rose, can you look after yourself for an hour or so? I've a mare about to foal...'

She laughed. 'Go. I'll be fine.'

'If you're sure? If you need me—'

'I'll whinny.'

His face relaxed into a smile. 'Actually, I think you'll find the telephone system is perfectly adequate.'

Alone, she turned back to the roses. Creamy white, perfect florist's blooms. She resisted the urge to count them; instead she thoughtfully riffled the satiny petals of a half-open bud with the edge of her thumb. The flowers were beautiful, but scentless, a sterile cliché without any real meaning.

And her thoughts wandered back to Prince Hassan al Rashid. The playboy prince was something of a cliché too. But those grey eyes suggested something very different behind the façade.

Prince Abdullah might woo her co-operation with his private jet and his roses, but it was Hassan who had her undivided attention.

CHAPTER TWO

'WHAT do you mean, you can't find him?' Hassan could barely contain his anger. 'He has bodyguards who watch him night and day—'

'He's given them the slip.' Partridge's voice echoed faintly on the satellite link. 'Apparently there's a girl involved—'

Of course there would be a girl. Damn the boy. And damn those blockheads who were supposed to look after him...

Except that he'd been twenty-four himself, once, centuries ago, and remembered only too well how it felt to live every waking moment under watchful eyes. Remembered just how easy it was to lose them when there was a girl...

'Find him, Partridge. Find him and bring him home. Tell him...' What? That he was sorry? That he understood? What good would that do? 'Tell him there isn't much time.'

'I'll do whatever is necessary, Excellency.'

Hassan stood at the entrance to his tent, Partridge's words ringing in his head. *Whatever is necessary...* His dying grandfather had used those words to him on the day he'd named his younger grandson, Faisal, his heir, and his nephew, Abdullah, as Regent. *Whatever is necessary for my country.* It had been an apology of sorts, but, hurting and angry at being dispossessed, he had

24

refused to understand and had behaved like the young
fool that he'd been.

Older, wiser, he understood that for a man to rule he
must first accept that the wishes of the heart must always be sacrificed to necessity.

In a few short weeks Faisal would be twenty-five,
and if his young half-brother was to take on the burden
of kingship he too would have to learn that lesson. And
quickly.

In the meantime something would have to be done
to disrupt Abdullah's attempt at coup by media. His
cousin might not encourage the press to come calling
at his door, but he understood its power, and he would
not let the chance slip to have someone like Rose
Fenton in his pocket.

She'd already been given the official grand tour of
the more fragrant parts of city, and it would be so easy
to be fooled into believing everything was wonderful if
you weren't looking too hard. And Abdullah had it in
his power to distract her in all manner of ways.

She might not succumb to the gifts, the gold and
pearls that would be showered upon her. It was unlikely—he had little faith in the myth of the crusading,
incorruptible journalist—but Abdullah had never been
a one-plan dictator. If money wouldn't do it, he had her
brother as a hostage to her co-operation.

Well, two could play at that game, and, although he
was sure she wouldn't take the same view of the situation, Hassan reasoned that he would actually be doing
Miss Fenton a favour if he took her out of circulation
for a while.

And dealing with her frantic family, the British

Foreign Office, the unkind comments of the British media, would give his cousin something more pressing to worry him than usurping Faisal's throne. It might even prompt him to bail out. While Abdullah enjoyed the tribute that went with his role as stand-in Head of State, he wasn't nearly so keen on the responsibilities that accompanied the role.

Partridge would doubtless be outraged, but, since his aide was clearly aware of the urgent necessity of doing whatever it took, he could be relied upon to keep his own counsel. In public, if not in private.

'Horse racing?' Rose helped herself to a slice of toast. It was six years since she'd been to a racetrack. It might not have been a deliberate decision, but she had always found some pressing reason to decline the many invitations to Ascot and Cheltenham that came her way. 'At night?'

'Under floodlights. It's cooler then. Especially in summer,' Tim added, then grinned. 'There'll be camel racing, too. Would you want to miss that?'

'Would I?' She pretended to think. 'Yes.'

For a moment she thought he was going to say something. Give her the 'it's been nearly six years' speech. He clearly thought better of it, because he shrugged and said, 'Well, it's up to you.' If he was disappointed by her decision he didn't let it show, and she could hardly believe that he was surprised. 'I have to be there for obvious reasons, but I can come back and pick you up afterwards.'

She glanced up from the careful application of butter to her toast. 'Pick me up?'

Tim indicated the square white envelope propped up against the marmalade. 'We've been invited out to dinner after the races.'

'Again?' Didn't anyone ever stay in for a pizza and a video in Ras al Hajar? 'Who by?'

'Simon Partridge.'

'Have I met him?' she asked, picking up the envelope and extracting a single sheet of paper. The handwriting was bold and strong. The note oddly formal. 'Simon Partridge requests the pleasure...'

'No, he's Prince Hassan's aide.'

About to plead tiredness, a headache, anything to get out of another formal evening, the night in with a video suddenly lost its appeal. She hadn't seen the playboy prince since he got off the plane. She'd looked for him, listened out for his name, but he appeared to have vanished from the face of the earth.

'You'll like him,' Tim said. She was sure her brother meant Simon Partridge rather than Hassan, but she didn't ask; she had the feeling that it would be wiser not to draw attention to her interest. 'He was desperately keen to meet you, but he's been out of town.'

'Really?' And then she laughed. 'Tell me, Tim, where do you go when you go "out of town" in Ras al Hajar?'

'Nowhere. That's the point. You leave civilisation behind.'

'I've done that.' She'd been in some very uncivilised places in the last few years. Too many. 'It's overrated.'

'The desert is different. Which is why, if you're someone like Hassan, the first thing you do when you get home is take your hounds and your hawks out into the desert and go hunting. And if you're his aide, you go with him.'

'I see.' What she saw was that if Simon Partridge was back in town, then so was Prince Hassan. 'Tell me about him. Simon Partridge. It's unusual for someone like Hassan to have a British aide, surely?'

'His grandfather had one and lived to tell the tale.'

'Did he?'

Tim frowned. 'Hassan's father. He was a Scot. Didn't I say?'

'No, you didn't.' Well, he hadn't. 'It explains a lot.'

Tim shrugged. 'Maybe he feels he can rely on Partridge one hundred per cent to be his man, with no divided tribal loyalties, no family feuds to get in the way.'

'A back to get in the way should someone feel like stabbing him in it?' she pondered. 'What does Simon Partridge get out of it?'

'Just a job. He's not Hassan's bodyguard. Partridge *was* in the army, but his Jeep got into a bit of an argument with a landmine and he was invalided out. His Colonel and Hassan were at school together...'

'Eton,' she murmured, without thinking.

'Where else?' Tim had assumed it was a question. 'Partridge, too.' He looked pleased at her apparent interest in his absent friend and Rose sighed, suspecting a little furtive matchmaking. 'So?' Tim retrieved the invitation. 'What shall I tell him?'

That was easy. The racing might be a non-starter, but Rose wasn't going to miss out on a chance to meet Hassan's aide. She handed him back the note. 'Tell him... Miss Fenton accepts...'

'Great.' The phone rang and Tim answered it, listened, then said, 'I'll be right there.' He was halfway to the door before he remembered Rose. 'Simon's number is on the note. Will you call him?'

'No problem.' She picked up the receiver, dialled the number. As it rang, she looked again at the bold cursive and decided Tim was right for once. She was sure she would like the owner of such a decisive hand.

'Yes?'

'Mr Partridge? Simon Partridge?'

There was the briefest pause. 'I believe I have the pleasure of speaking to Miss Rose Fenton.'

'Er, yes.' She laughed. 'How did you know?'

'If I told you I was psychic?' the voice offered.

'I wouldn't believe you.'

'And you would be right not to. Your voice is unmistakable, Miss Fenton.'

While Simon Partridge sounded rather older than she had expected from Tim's description of him, his voice was low, deeply authoritative, velvet on steel. Not that she was about to drool into the phone.

'That's because I talk too much,' she replied crisply. 'Tim's had to rush off to the stables, but he asked me to ring you and say that we're delighted to accept your invitation to dinner this evening.'

'I have no doubt that the delight will be all mine.'

His formality was so very…foreign. She wondered how long he had been in Ras al Hajar. She'd assumed it was a fairly recent thing, but maybe not. 'You know he has to go to the races first, of course—'

'Everyone goes to the races, Miss Fenton. There is nothing else to do in Ras al Hajar. You will be there?'

'Well…'

'You must come.'

Must she? 'Yes,' she said, rapidly changing her mind. She rather thought she must. After all, she reasoned, if everyone went to the races, Hassan would be there. 'Yes, I'm looking forward to it.' And suddenly she was. Very much.

'Until this evening, Miss Fenton.'

'Until then, Mr Partridge,' she replied. And she put down the receiver feeling just a touch breathless.

Hassan switched off the cellphone that had been purchased in the souk that morning and registered in an entirely fictitious name and tossed it on the divan. Beyond the opening of the huge black tent he could see the lush palm grove watered by the small streams that ran from the craggy mountainous border country. In spring it was paradise on earth. He had the feeling that Rose Fenton might not view it in quite the same way.

'Come home quickly, Faisal,' he murmured. At the sound of his voice the hound at his feet rose and pushed a long silky head against his hand.

Rose was thoroughly dissatisfied with her small wardrobe. She'd felt like an absolute dowd at the embassy cocktail party. She'd assumed that it would be smart but casual. Tim had been absolutely no help and in the end she'd decided on her crush-proof go-anywhere little black dress. In the event, of course, all the other women had taken the opportunity to wear their latest designer creations, leaving the black dress looking as if it had

already been around the world and back again. Well, it
had.

She hadn't anticipated so much socialising, and besides, she had nothing that could possibly cover an evening outdoors at the races followed by a private dinner.

She would normally have asked her hostess what
would be suitable. But there was no hostess, and something about Simon Partridge had precluded that kind of
informal chattiness. It was the same something that
urged her to make a real effort, pull out all the stops,
and she decided to wear the *shalwar kameez* that she'd
been given on a trip to Pakistan and packed in the hope
of an interview with the Regent. Something she'd been
doing her best to avoid ever since she'd arrived, although even she had begun to run out of convincing
excuses.

The trousers were cut from heavy slub silk in a dull
mossy shade, the tunic a shade or two lighter and the
hand-embroidered silk chiffon scarf paler still. She
should have worn it to the embassy.

'Wow!' Tim's reaction was unexpected. He didn't
usually notice what anyone wore. 'You look stunning.'

'That's worrying. I suddenly get the feeling that
everyone else will be wearing jeans.'

'Does it matter? You're going to absolutely knock
Simon's eyes out.'

'I'm not sure that's the effect I'm striving for, Tim.'
Remembering the effect of his voice on her ability to
breathe, she thought she might just be kidding herself.
'At least not until I know him better.'

'In that outfit he'll definitely want to get to know you

better.' He glanced at his watch. 'We'd better go. Got everything?'

'Hanky, safety pin, ten pence for the telephone,' she said solemnly. Her cellphone, tape recorder, notebook and pen went without saying. And she didn't say anything because she had the feeling they would make her brother uneasy.

Tim laughed. 'I'd forgotten the way Mum used to say that.' He put his arm beneath her elbow and helped her up into the Range Rover.

'How far is it?'

'Oh, just a couple of miles beyond the stables. Once you get through these low hills there's a good flat piece of ground that's perfect for racing.' He pulled a face as they bumped over the rough track. 'Sorry about this. The Emir's had a dual-carriageway road laid from town, but this way's much quicker for us.'

'Hey, this is "Front-line" Fenton you're talking to. A few bumps aren't going to... Oh, look out!'

A pale riderless horse leapt from a low bluff and landed in front of them, turning to rear up in front of the car, mane flying, hooves pawing at the air. Tim swung to avoid it, throwing the car into a sideways skid that seemed to go on for ever on the loose gravel.

'It's one of Abdullah's horses,' he said, as he brought the Range Rover under control. 'Someone's going to be in trouble—' The moment they stopped, he flung open the door and leapt down. 'Sorry, but I'll have to try and catch it.'

'Can I do anything?' She turned as he opened the tailgate and took out a rope halter.

'No. Yes. Use the car phone to call the stables. Ask them to send a horsebox.'

'Where?'

'Just say between the villa and the stables; they'll find us.'

The interior light had not come on and she reached up, clicked the switch, but nothing happened. She shrugged, lifted the phone, but there was no dial tone. Great. She picked up her bag and dug out the new mobile phone that Gordon had included in the carrier with the book and the cuttings. It was small, very powerful and did just about everything except play the national anthem, but she wasn't confident enough with it to press buttons in the dark, so slid down from her seat to check it out in the headlights. Her feet had just touched the ground when the headlights went out.

She could hear her brother, some distance off, gentling the nervous horse, hear the scrabbling of hooves against the rough ground as the lovely creature danced away from him. Then that sound, too, abruptly stopped as the horse found sand.

It was so quiet, so dark in the shadow of the bluff. There was no moon, but the stars were brilliant, undimmed by light pollution, and the sand reflected the faintest silvery shimmer against which everything else was jet-black.

A shadow detached itself from the darkness.

'Tim?'

But it wasn't her brother. Even before she turned she knew it wasn't him. Tim had smelt faintly of aftershave, was wearing a light-coloured jacket. This man had no scent that she could discern and he was dressed from head to foot in a robe of a blackness so dense that it absorbed light rather than reflecting it. Even his face was concealed in a black *keffiyeh* worn so that nothing but his eyes were visible.

His eyes were all she needed to see.

It was Hassan. Despite the charge of fear that fixed her to the spot, despite the adrenalin-driven panicky race of her heart, she knew him. But this was not the urbane Prince boarding a private jet in expensive Italian tailoring; this was not Hassan in playboy prince mode.

This was the man promised by granite-grey eyes, deep, dangerous and totally in command, and something warned her that he wasn't about to ask if she needed help.

Before she could do more than half turn to run, before she could even think about shouting a warning to her brother, he'd clamped his hand over her mouth. Then, with his free arm flung around her, he lifted her clear of the ground as he pulled her hard against his body. Hard enough for the curved weight of the dagger at his waist to dig into her ribs.

Definitely not from the local branch of auto rescue.

She might have done a self-defence course but so apparently had he, because he knew all the moves. Her elbows were immobilised, and with her feet off the ground she had no platform from which to launch a counter-move. Not that it would do her any good. She might make the high ground, but what then? There was nowhere to run to and, although she couldn't see anyone else, she doubted that he was alone.

She struggled anyway.

He simply tightened his grip and waited, and after a

moment she stopped. There was no point in wearing herself out unnecessarily.

When she was quite still except for the unnaturally swift rise and fall of her breast as she tried to regain her breath, he finally spoke. 'I would be grateful if you did not shout, Miss Fenton,' he said, very quietly. 'I have no wish to hurt your brother.' And his voice was like his hand, like his eyes, hard, uncompromising, not playing games.

He knew who she was, then. This wasn't some random snatch. No. Of course it wasn't. It might have been some days since they'd exchanged that momentary glance on the plane that had brought her to Ras al Hajar, but she'd heard the voice much more recently. Heard it insisting that she must go to the races. And she had blithely assured him that she would be there. That had been the reason for the invitation; he'd wanted to be sure she would be there so he could plan exactly where and when to abduct her.

Not Simon Partridge, then. But Hassan. She realised that she wasn't as surprised as she might have been. The voice was a much better fit.

But what did he want? Just because she'd read a few pages of *The Sheik* in an idle moment, that didn't mean she subscribed to the fantasy. She didn't think for a minute that he was about to carry her off into the desert for the purposes of ravishment. She was a journalist, and not given much to flights of fancy. And why would he bother when, with the click of his fingers, he could bring just about any woman he desired to his side?

'Well?' He was offering her a choice? Not much of one. She nodded, once, promising her silence.

'Thank you.' The formal courtesy was unmistakable.
As if she had had any choice but surrender! But, as if
to prove that he was a gentleman, Hassan immediately
removed his hand from her mouth, set her feet to the
ground, eased his grip on her. Maybe he was so used
to obedience that it didn't occur to him that she
wouldn't keep quiet, keep still. Or maybe it didn't matter all that much. There was only Tim, after all, and
with a sudden sense of dread she recalled the sudden
silence.

'Where is Tim? What have you done with him?' she
demanded as she spun back to face him, her own voice
hushed in the absolute still of the desert night. Hushed!
She should be screaming her head off...

'Nothing. He's still chasing after Abdullah's favourite stallion.' The eyes gleamed. 'I imagine he'll be gone
some time. This way, Miss Fenton.' Her eyes, quickly
adjusting to the darkness, saw the uncompromising
shape of a Land Rover waiting in the shadows. Not one
of the plush, upmarket jobs that her brother drove, but
the basic kind that took to hard terrain like a duck to
water. The kind used by military men the world over.

Far more practical than a horse, she didn't doubt, any
more than she doubted that she would go wherever he
was taking her. Her only alternative was to run for it,
try and dodge him in the rocky outcrops of the rising
ground behind her. As if he anticipated she might try
it, Hassan tightened his hold and urged her towards the
waiting vehicle.

Despite the prickle of fear that was goosing her flesh,
all her journalist instincts were on red alert. But, although her curiosity was intense, she didn't want him

to think she was going willingly. 'You've got to be kidding,' she said, and dug in her heels.

'Kidding?' He repeated the word as if he didn't understand it. Then he raised his head, looked beyond her. The moon was rising, and as she turned she saw the dark silhouette of her brother in the distance. He had managed to get the head rope on the stallion and was leading him quietly back towards the Range Rover, completely oblivious to her plight, to the danger he was walking into.

Hassan had seriously underestimated his skill, his empathy with even the most difficult of horses, and, realising it, he swore beneath his breath. 'I don't have time to argue.'

She wasn't about to let Tim walk into trouble, but even as she drew a ragged breath to shout a warning she was enveloped in blackness. Real blackness, the kind that made starlight look like day, and she was wrapped, parcelled, bundled, lifted off her feet and slung over his shoulder.

Far too late she stopped being the cool correspondent, absorbing every last detail for her report, and began to struggle in dreadful earnest. Too late she realised she should have yelled when she'd had the chance. Not for help, since that would surely be pointless, but to make sure that Tim called her news editor to tell him what had happened.

She kicked furiously in an effort to free her head, not wasting her breath in shouting, because her voice wouldn't make it beyond the confines of the heavy cloth. But although her feet were free to inflict whatever damage she could manage they appeared to make no impression upon her captor. If only she could free her hands! But they were pinned uselessly to her sides... Well, not quite uselessly. One them was still gripping the little mobile phone. She almost smiled. The mobile. Well, that was all right, then. She'd call the news desk herself...

Then she was dumped unceremoniously on the floor of the truck, and even through the thick muffling cloth she could hear the sound of an engine, smell hot diesel oil. Diesel oil? Where were the horses? Where was the glamour?

Right now, according to the book she'd read on the plane, she should be racing across the desert crushed against her captor's hard body and struggling desperately for her honour...

She almost laughed. Times had certainly changed. Her honour was the last thing on her mind. She'd been kidnapped and all she could think about was calling in the story.

Well, not quite all. There had been a moment as she'd been crushed against Hassan's chest, with his hand clamped across her mouth and his gaze locked with hers, when swooning would have been very easy. And it didn't need a particularly vivid imagination to picture his body hard against hers, holding her tightly as she continued to fight him even as the Land Rover sped away.

Only three days ago she'd been joking about being swept off by a desert prince. Bad mistake. It wasn't a bit funny. She was being jolted hard against the Land Rover floor and, as if he realised it, her captor rolled so that he was beneath her, taking the worst of it.

Although whether lying on top of a man hell-bent on abduction could be described as an improvement... But with his arm still clamped about her, she didn't have any choice.

Maybe it would be wiser to stop struggling, though, put the fantasy firmly from her mind, ignore the intimacy of their tangled legs and try and work out what on earth Hassan thought he was doing. Ask herself why he had taken such a crazy risk.

It would be easier to think without the suffocating weight of the cloak depriving her of her senses, without his arms wrapped tightly about her.

She supposed she should be afraid. Poor Tim would be frantic. Then there was her mother. So much for the constant nagging to be prepared. For the first time in her life she had a real use for the safety pin, could have jabbed it into His Highness's thigh hard enough to make him seriously regret grabbing her, maybe even hard enough to make him let go so that she could throw off the covering.

Unfortunately her handbag, containing the pin, was sitting on the floor of Tim's Range Rover. Along with the clean hanky and the ten pence piece for the emergency telephone call.

This situation certainly fell into the emergency telephone call category, although how many public telephones was she likely to find in the desert? Her mother hadn't thought of that one.

Still, when she found out that her daughter was missing, Pam Fenton would spend far more than ten pence on the telephone giving the Foreign Office hell.

If she found out her daughter was missing. Rose had

the feeling that her disappearance would be kept out of
the news if Abdullah could manage it. And he probably
could. Tim wouldn't be too hard to convince that her
safety depended upon it. And the embassy would do
whatever they thought was most likely to achieve her
safe return. Just as well she had the mobile, then;
Gordon would never forgive her for failing to turn in
this scoop.

Oh, Lord! Whatever had happened to her fright-or-
flight mechanism? She wasn't afraid; she wasn't planning escape. The primary emotion flowing through her
system was indignation at the unromantic manner of her
abduction.

She should just be grateful that Hassan hadn't hurt
her, that he hadn't tied her up, or gagged her. Well, he
hadn't needed to. She hadn't yelled when she could
have, should have. Even now she was lying still and
doing nothing at all to make life difficult for the man.
That was because curiosity was running indignation a
close second.

What did Hassan *want*?

Not just a cosy chat. If he'd wanted that he could
have knocked on the villa door any time and she'd have
been happy to offer him a cup of tea and a chocolate
digestive. It was the way they did it in Chelsea. Maybe
they did things differently in Ras al Hajar.

Or maybe he had an entirely different agenda.

Think, Rose! Think! What possible reason could
Hassan al Rashid have for kidnapping her? What reason
did anyone have?

Ransom? Ridiculous.

Sex? There was a momentary wobble somewhere

low in her abdomen at the thought, then she dismissed the idea as errant nonsense.

Could this be the playboy prince's idea of a joke? After all, his cousin the Regent would be seriously ticked off by the kind of publicity this little escapade would generate, and rumour suggested there was no love lost between the two men. She could just imagine the headlines, the news bulletins...

Suddenly everything clicked into place. That had to be it. Headlines. This was no joke. Hassan wanted Ras al Hajar in the news. More than that, he wanted to embarrass Abdullah...

Quite suddenly, she lost her temper. Drat the story! Here she was, wrapped up like a parcel of washing, her bones rattling like stones in a cup, and all because Hassan thought it would be amusing to irritate his cousin with bad headlines and she happened to be a handy source of aggravation.

She felt aggrieved. Seriously aggrieved. She was a woman. Not film star material, maybe, but she had all the right bits in all the right places. Her hair... All right, she might have personal reservations about her hair, but there was no doubt that it was an unmissable shade of red. Her eyes might be plain old brown, but they did the job and came complete with the regulation set of lashes. Her nose... Oh, what the heck. She stopped the inventory and, digging her knees into whatever part of his anatomy happened to be in the way, she heaved herself up and back.

Surprise, or maybe pain, together with the serendipitous lurching of the Land Rover as it raced over the rough terrain, combined to loosen Hassan's grip. She

just had time to fling off the cloak before he recovered,
caught her and pinned her against the floor. And, as she
dragged great gulps of fresh air into her lungs, she was
once again staring up into those dangerous grey eyes.

Her situation was not lost upon her. She was vulnerable and utterly at the mercy of a man she did not know,
whose motives were less than clear. One of them had
better say something. And quickly.

'When you ask a girl to dinner, Your Highness, you
really, really mean it, don't you?'

CHAPTER THREE

'DINNER?' Hassan repeated.

Rose blew away an errant curl that was threatening to make her sneeze. 'That *was* you, this morning? "Simon Partridge requests the pleasure..." Tell me, does Mr Partridge know that you've taken his name in vain?'

'Ah.'

Ah? That was it? 'Well?' she demanded. 'Is dinner off? I warn you, I don't do well on bread and water. I'm going to need feeding—'

'Dinner has been arranged, Miss Fenton, but I'm afraid you'll have to accept Mr Partridge's regrets. He's at present out of the country and, in answer to your first question, no, he has no idea that I have used his name. He is, in fact, entirely blameless in this affair.'

The significance of that was not lost on her. Investigations would quickly establish that this was a carefully planned snatch, that someone had used a known friendship to ensure her presence at the races. But when the authorities checked out the telephone number on that invitation, she just knew that it would lead absolutely nowhere.

'Well,' she said, after a moment, 'I hope he gives you a piece of his mind when he does find out.'

'I think you can rely on that.'

Actually, Rose had been planning to give him a piece

43

of her own mind, but Hassan's voice did not encourage liberties and she thought that it might be wiser to leave it to Simon Partridge. Wherever he was. She hoped he wouldn't be away long. The sneeze threatened again and, inspired, she changed tack. 'You didn't have to bundle me up like that, you know.' She gave a little cough. 'I've not been well.'

'So I've been told.' He didn't sound totally convinced by her act, and she realised that playing for sympathy would get her nowhere. 'You seem to be managing to have a good time, though. Personally, I wouldn't have thought that a busy round of cocktail parties, receptions, public relations tours of the city were at all good for you—'

'Oh, I *see*! You're doing me a *kindness*. You've abducted me so that I shouldn't over-exert myself.'

'That is a point of view.' Hassan's eyes creased in a smile. It was not a reassuring smile, however. 'I'm afraid my cousin has no thought but his own pleasure—'

'And mine. He told me so himself.' She had not been entirely convinced by that, either. Prince Abdullah seemed terribly keen that she should get a very positive image of the country. The curtained windows of the limousine that had taken her around the city at high speed had, she felt sure, hidden a multitude of sins.

She'd been planning to put on one of the all-enveloping black *abbayahs* worn by the local women and, heavily veiled to disguise her red hair, have a closer look around on her own. Not that she had proposed to involve Tim in her little outing. She strongly suspected he would disapprove.

'And as for standing about in the night air at the race course,' Hassan continued. 'Most unwise. It's almost certain to lead to a relapse.'

Except that until she'd spoken to him she hadn't planned on going anywhere near the race course. She didn't bother to mention it, though. She didn't want him to know he'd had anything to do with her changing her mind. 'Your concern is most touching.'

'Your appreciation is noted. You are in Ras al Hajar for rest and relaxation and it will be my pleasure to see that you get it.'

His pleasure? She didn't care for the sound of that. 'Prince Hassan al Rashid, the perfect host,' she responded sarcastically, easing her shoulder from the hard floor of the Land Rover in as pointed a manner as she could manage, considering that she was practically being sat on.

The gesture was wasted. All she got for her trouble was the slightest bow of his head as he acknowledged his name. 'I do my best.' He ignored her snort of disbelief. 'You came to my country for pleasure, a holiday. A little romance, perhaps, if the book you were reading on the plane is anything to judge by?'

Oh, good grief! If he was into fulfilling holiday fantasies, she was in big trouble. She swallowed. 'At least *The Sheik* had style.'

'Style?'

'A Land Rover is no substitute for a stallion.' She realised she was letting her mouth run away with her. Nerves, no doubt. She might refuse to admit to fear but she was entitled to be a little nervous. 'Black as night, with the temper of the devil,' she prompted. 'That's the more usual mode of transport for desert abductees. I have to tell you that I feel short-changed.'

'Do you?' He sounded surprised by that. Who could blame him? 'Regrettably our destination is too far for us to ride there doubled up on a horse.' His eyes smiled, and this time there was no doubt about it; there was not a thing to be reassured about. 'Especially when you've been unwell.' *Oh, very funny.* 'I will make a note for the future, however.'

'Oh, please. Don't trouble yourself.' She attempted to sit up, but he did not move.

'The ground is rough, I wouldn't want you thrown about. You'll be safer lying down.'

With the length of his body covering hers? Did she have any choice? But he was probably right. It would be safer...

What? She couldn't believe she was even thinking that! This man might fulfil all the criteria of the fantasy but that was all it was, a fantasy. He'd kidnapped her and she was far from safe.

She swallowed. Tried to gather her wits. The network briefed staff on this kind of situation before sending them to dangerous parts of the world. She knew that she was supposed to keep the man talking. Make him see her as a person.

The way he was looking at her, the fact that his legs straddled her, that his hips were pressed firmly against her abdomen suggested that he could do little other than see her as a person. A *female* person.

All the more reason to talk. 'You've gone to a lot of trouble for my company. If you wanted to talk to me, why didn't you come and join me on the plane? Or call at my brother's house—'

Maybe he was getting the same thoughts, because without warning he moved, shifting to her side so that he was lying alongside her, eyeing her warily. 'You knew who I was, didn't you? Back there?'

Instantly. She had no intention of flattering him, though. 'I shouldn't think too many of the local bandits went to an English public school. And very few of them have grey eyes.' Even in the darkness, his eyes had been unmistakable. 'And of course there was your voice. I heard that just a few hours ago. If you'd wanted to remain anonymous, you should have sent one of your henchmen to capture me.'

'That would have been unthinkable.'

'You mean your men mustn't handle the goods? That's very possessive of you.' And distinctly unnerving. Or it would be if she wasn't already thoroughly unnerved.

'You are very cool, Miss Fenton.' He reached up to unwrap the *keffiyeh*. The moonlight was shining through the windscreen and into the rear of the truck so that his face was all black and white angles. Harsher than she remembered. 'But you shouldn't be deceived by my education. My mother is an Arab, my father was Highland Scots. I am not one of your English gentlemen.'

No. She felt, finally, a tiny quiver of something closer to fear than she cared to admit to, even in her head. Closer to fear. But not quite fear. She moistened her dry lips and refused to back down. 'Well, I suppose that's something,' she said, with reckless bravado.

There was a flash of white teeth in the darkness before he said, 'Are you really so brave?'

Sure she was. Everyone knew that. Rose 'Front-line' Fenton didn't know the meaning of the word fear. Not much. But this had nothing to do with courage. She'd recognised the danger at twenty feet as he'd stepped on the plane. At twenty inches his magnetism was likely to prove fatal, but it was entirely possible that she would die happy.

It was just as well that the moonlight did not reach her face. She would not like him to read her thoughts.

'Have you no interest in where I'm taking you?' he demanded.

The noisy rattling had stopped a little while ago and they were making speed on a good road. But which one? And in which direction? 'If I asked you, would you tell me?'

'No,' he snapped. Her bravado, it seemed, was beginning to irritate him. 'But be assured I have not carried you off for the pleasure of your conversation, although I have no doubt it will be an unexpected bonus.'

A bonus? To what?

'I wouldn't count on it.' Oh, heck. The golden rule in situations like this was listen and learn, but she couldn't help it. She just couldn't be all girly and pathetic, apparently not even to save her life. Or anything else. Well, that was how myths were made. With a big mouth.

But, for all her bluff, her heart stepped up a gear. Could she be wrong? Could it be that he regularly carried off visiting females? 'Tell me, do you do this sort of thing often?' she asked. Well, that was what she did.

Asked questions. 'Do you have a harem of women like me stashed away in some desert encampment?'

'How many women like you could one man stand?' he demanded, finally exasperated with her and clearly far from amused that she could conceive of such an idea. That pleased her. Whatever he had in mind for her, she would like to be an original.

But he was waiting for her answer. His eyes gleamed darkly as he waited for her to ask why he had carried her off, what he intended to do with her. Unbridled curiosity was undoubtedly her greatest strength, but it was also a weakness. She just never knew when to stop. And her curiosity about this man had been aroused long before she'd set eyes upon him.

His face was above her in the harsh white moonlight, hard planes and dark shadows. His expression was closed, his eyes steeply hooded. She didn't want him to hide from her, wanted no shadows, and without thinking she raised her hand to his face.

Startled by her touch, he pulled back an inch or two. But where could he go? In the rear of the Land Rover he was as much her prisoner as she was his, and, emboldened, she flattened her palm against his cheek, felt the rough stubble of an hours-old beard. This time he held fast, submitted to her exploring touch as she rubbed the side of her thumb along the hard edge of his jaw. She shouldn't be doing this, but there was an excitement about the danger, and as she trailed the tips of her fingers over the chiselled lines of his lips she felt him swallow.

In that brief moment she was the predator, not

Hassan, and in the darkness she smiled and gave him her answer.

'If a man was fortunate enough to have one woman like me, Your Highness, I would make it my life's work to ensure that he wanted no other.' For a moment she let her fingers linger against his mouth, and then she took them away.

Hassan bit back a caustic retort. What could he say? He believed her. And he recognised it not as an invitation but as a warning. What a woman! She hadn't turned a single strand of that beautiful red hair when he seized her. She had not cried out when she might have, but had defied him, was still defying him with her words and with her body, even though she had no idea what her fate might be.

It was fortunate indeed for Rose Fenton that he was nothing like the bitter, twisted man in the old novel she had been reading, or he would have been seriously tempted to put her courage to the test.

If he were honest with himself, he'd admit that he was tempted anyway. She was quite different from any woman he had ever met. She wasn't coy, she wasn't flirtatious, she wasn't afraid...or maybe it was just that she'd had more practice in hiding fear than most women of his acquaintance.

He found himself wanting to reassure her, but suspected she would despise him for such dishonesty. She would be right too. And he realised that it would be wise to put some distance between them.

He had never intended to keep her so personally his captive. For one brief, exhilarating moment he'd even thought that she would come freely, that she could ride up front with him. Maybe if she hadn't seen help so close at hand she would have come quietly.

But the moment had been lost and she was hard to read. The last thing he wanted was to have her throwing herself out of the vehicle. Not at the speed they were travelling. He moved to his knees, gathered the discarded cloak, wadded it into a pillow, then hesitated, unwilling to touch her, risk a repeat of the sizzling impact of her skin against his. But the Land Rover lurched and rattled as they took to the desert again, shaking them both, and, gritting his teeth, he cupped her neck in his hand.

His fingers were cool, firm, insistent against the sensitive skin of her neck, and for a moment Rose thought he was taking her at her word. 'Lift your head,' he said as she resisted, his voice as firm as his touch. 'Try and make yourself comfortable.' And he pushed the cloak beneath her head. 'We've some way to go.'

'How far?' she asked, as he moved away to sit crosslegged against the side of the Land Rover, between her and the rear door. Barring any attempt at escape. Did he think she was that foolhardy? When she had first been snatched she might have thought of it, but not now. She would be lost, hurt, and it would be a long cold night in the desert before she could hope for rescue. 'How far?' she repeated. Hassan's look suggested she was pushing her luck. 'Won't there be people looking for us by now?' she pressed. Helicopters, Jeeps...they could follow the tyre marks until they reached the road, but not until it was light. Nine or ten hours from now at the earliest.

'Maybe.' He glanced at his wristwatch, black, like

everything else he wore, against the pallor of his wrist. 'Your brother has no phone, no way of calling for help and he's hampered by Abdullah's favourite stallion. Will he put you or the horse first?'

'You broke into Tim's car and disconnected the car phone?' she asked, avoiding a direct answer. 'Removed the bulb from the interior light?'

'Not personally.'

No. There was only one person who could have done that. Khalil, who smiled and bowed and served her brother with such eagerness.

'And you let loose Abdullah's horse.' Personally or not, the intent had been his. Hassan's preparations had been thorough, Rose realised. And using the horse had been particularly clever. Tim would never leave one of Abdullah's valuable horses running wild where it might get hurt. She hadn't been in Ras al Hajar for long, but she had quickly realised that no one would be foolish enough to steal it.

'And let loose Abdullah's horse,' he agreed. 'What will your brother do?' Hassan persisted.

'What would you do?' she countered.

'I would have no choice. I would come after you.' With murder on his mind, she had no doubt. She sensed rather than saw him shrug. 'The horse will return to his stable as soon as he's hungry.'

'I expect that's what Tim will do, then,' she said.

'But he's an Englishman.'

'An English gentleman to his boot straps,' she agreed. 'But does that preclude the passionate response?'

'I would anticipate reason rather than passion, but you know him. Is your brother a passionate man?'

How tempting to say that her brother would come after her and kill the man who'd dishonoured her. Perhaps it was fortunate that Tim was exactly the reasoned, sensible man Hassan imagined. Not that she was going to reassure him.

'I've absolutely no idea what Tim's reaction will be,' she said truthfully, banging the makeshift pillow into a more comfortable shape and deliberately turning away from him. 'I've never been kidnapped before.'

By the time the truck finally shuddered to a halt, Rose was stiff in every limb. They had left the smooth, fast highway long since, and the rattling of the chassis, the thrumming of the powerful engine had combined with tension to give her a seriously bad headache. She didn't move even when the rear door was flung open.

'Miss Fenton?' Hassan had jumped down and was now inviting her to descend under her own steam, which suggested there was nowhere she could run for help. Well, she had expected nothing else. The fact that his voice was gentler than before did nothing to help. 'We have arrived.'

'Thanks,' she said, not looking up, not moving, 'but I'm not stopping.'

There was a brief exclamation of irritation. 'Stay there, then, stubborn woman. Stay and freeze.' There was a brief pause, presumably while he waited for her to see sense. In answer she pulled the cloak from beneath her head and covered herself with it. He swore...at least she assumed he was swearing; why else

would he do it under his breath? She didn't intend to
be prissy about it, after all, she hadn't planned to make
his day. But his anger had nothing to do with her declaration of independence. 'You're shivering.'

Mmm. The truck had stopped shaking, but she
hadn't. It wasn't anything to do with the cold, though.
It was the kind of uncontrollable shivering that started
after an accident, the result of shock. She'd had sufficient time to regret her show of bravado while her mind
had been taking her on a tour of the realities of her
situation. Shock seemed about right.

Maybe if she'd screamed, cried, gibbered with fear
when he'd grabbed her, Hassan would have thought
twice about carrying her off, whatever his reason. In
her experience men would do almost anything to avoid
that kind of thing. Unfortunately she didn't have much
practice in weeping hysterics.

So, no tears, no hysterics. She had even resisted, with
difficulty, the temptation to press the call button on her
telephone. The Land Rover was dark and noisy, but
Hassan had been close enough to hear if she'd tried to
call for help. She had to save the phone for a moment
when she could be sure that she wouldn't be overheard.

Maybe she shouldn't even do that, but save the battery for an emergency, although she preferred not to
think how much worse things could get. So she had
tucked the telephone down in the seam pocket of her
trousers where, with any luck, it would not be found.

She felt the rocking movement of the truck as Hassan
stepped up beside her. 'Come on,' he said. 'You've
done more than enough to justify your reputation.' He
didn't wait for further argument but gathered her up,

cloak and all, and, holding her close, carried her across the sand.

She considered protesting that she could walk perfectly well by herself, but in the end decided to save her breath. At five foot ten she was no lightweight. Maybe he'd put his back out carrying her. It would be no more than he deserved.

She saw the flicker of firelight, the shadowy shapes of men and palm trees against the night sky, and then she was inside one of those huge black tents that she had seen in some television documentary.

There was a brief glimpse of a lamplit room furnished with rugs and a divan before he elbowed aside a heavy drape and put her down on a large bed. A bed! She swung her legs to the floor and, clutching the cloak about her, stood up with a speed that sent the blood rushing from her head. She swayed and he caught her, held her for a moment, then lowered her back onto the bed, lifted her feet, removed her shoes.

That was it. Shoes were far enough.

'Go away,' she said, through gritted teeth. 'Just go away and leave me alone.'

Hassan ignored her, dropping her shoes beside the bed. He remained at her side, eyes narrowed as he watched her. And Rose felt the colour flush rapidly back to her cheeks. Apparently satisfied, he nodded, took a step back.

'You'll find hot water, everything you need through there,' he said, indicating yet another room beyond more thick dark hangings. 'Come through as soon as you've freshened up and we'll eat.' And with that he swung round and disappeared into the living apartment.

Eat! He expected her to tamely wash and brush up and sit down to eat a civilised meal with him?

She was outraged.

But she was also hungry.

With a shrug of resignation, she sat up and looked about her. This might be a tent, this might be camping, but, rather like the private jet, it was not as she recognised it. The room was hung with richly worked cloth, furnished with antique brass-bound campaign furniture, and a large trunk that she guessed doubled as a dressing table.

She put her feet to the floor, felt the smooth silk of the carpet beneath her feet. It was warmer inside and she threw off the cloak, padded across to the trunk and lifted the lid. As she'd suspected there was a shallow tray containing a mirror, brushes, combs. There were other things. Things that brought the tremor back to her fingers.

There were fresh supplies of the make-up she wore, a jar of her favourite moisturising cream, the sunblock she used. The man had done his homework. He wanted her to be comfortable. Which might have been heart-warming except that it suggested her stay might be prolonged. Which was anything but.

The bathroom was similarly equipped with shampoo and soap that were familiar friends. She poured hot water from a jug into the basin, washed her hands and face, all her suspicions about Khalil confirmed. Who else would be able to disconnect the telephone in the Range Rover, remove the light bulb without suspicion? Not that she blamed the young man. In a country where loyalty was first and always to the tribe, the outsider would always be at a disadvantage.

A fact Hassan had discovered for himself when he'd been passed over for the throne.

She returned to the dressing table, freshened her make-up, combed her hair, brushed the dust from her *shalwar kameez*. Then she picked up the long silk chiffon scarf. About to loop it about her throat, leaving the ends to trail below the hem of her tunic, the way she had worn it earlier, she changed her mind. Instead she draped it over her head, modestly covering her hair in the traditional style. Only then did she join her insistent host.

Hassan raked his fingers through his hair as he paced the rug. He'd expected tears. He'd expected hysterics. He'd been prepared for them. What he hadn't expected was the kind of in-your-face defiance that dared him to do his worst even when her teeth were chattering with delayed reaction shock.

What on earth was he going to do with her? She'd have to be watched night and day or she'd probably kill herself trying to get back to town.

It would have been easier at the fort, where there were doors with locks. But also much harder.

Too many people came and went there, and not all of them could be relied upon. It would have been much more difficult to keep her presence a secret. Out here, with a few picked men, men he would trust with his life, men he would trust with *her* life, that would not be a problem.

Out here he had relied on distance and the desert to

keep her his prisoner. His first encounter with Rose Fenton suggested that it wouldn't be so easy. So he'd have to offer something to make her want to stay. Something important.

As he reached the edge of the rug and turned the hangings were pushed aside, and his breath caught at the sight of her. In the darkness he hadn't seen what she was wearing when he'd seized her. He'd assumed she would be dressed in something a modern western woman would consider suitable for an evening at the races to be followed by dinner with a man she did not know but who might be worth the effort. Something dressy. Modern. Sharp. The kind of clothes worn by the kind of woman who'd travelled the world, risked all kinds of danger for her job.

The *shalwar kameez* was beautiful, but unexpectedly demure. The long chiffon scarf draped over her vivid red curls was exactly the kind of covering his half-sisters, his aunts, his mother would have worn at a mixed family gathering.

It was a shock to see her wearing something like that. It made him feel as if he had somehow violated her, and after that first still moment, when movement had seemed beyond him, he crossed swiftly to pull back a chair for her.

She didn't immediately take it, but glanced about her, taking in the brass-bound map chest, the fold-out travelling desk. 'When you go camping,' she said, 'you certainly do it in style.'

Demure, but still full of fire. 'You have a problem with that?'

'Who, me?' She crossed to take the chair he held for

her, sat down with all the poise of his Scottish grandmother at a vicarage tea party. 'Hell, no, Your
Highness,' she said, dispelling the image as quickly as
she'd provoked it. And she took a linen napkin from
the table, flicked it open and laid it on her lap. 'If I
have to be abducted, I'd just as soon it was done by a
man with the good sense to install an *en suite* bathroom
in his tent.'

'I am not a Highness,' he snapped. 'Yours or anyone
else's. Call me Hassan.'

'You want to be friends?' She laughed. Laughed! A
few minutes ago she'd been shivering in his arms, her
teeth chattering.

'No, Miss Fenton, I want to eat.'

He crossed to the entrance to the tent and barked a
swift command before turning to rejoin her. His head
was bare, revealing the thick thatch of hair that, against
the unrelieved blackness of their surroundings, was not
as dark as she remembered.

In the lamplight a hint of red betrayed his Scottish
father's Highland roots. But everything else, the black
robes bound with a heavy sash, the *khanjar* he wore at
his waist, was from another world. The ornate filigree
silver scabbard was old and very beautiful, but the knife
it held was not an ornament.

It would be easy to forget that, to think of Hassan as
civilised. She was certain he could be charming. But
she wasn't fooled. There was a streak of steel through
the man, tempered in fire every bit as hot as the one
that had tempered the blade of his dagger. Sense told
her it would be wiser not to stir up the embers. Her

nature suggested she would be unable to resist the temptation. But not yet. Not yet.

They ate in silence. Lamb broiled over an open fire, rice spiced with saffron and pine nuts. Rose had thought she wouldn't be hungry, but the food was good and there was nothing to be gained from a hunger strike. It would be far wiser to conserve all her strength.

Afterwards one of Hassan's men brought dates and almonds and thin desert coffee scented with cardamom.

She took an almond, nibbled on it while Hassan drank his coffee and stared out into the darkness. 'Are you going to tell me what this is all about?' she asked eventually. He didn't move. Said nothing. 'I only ask because my brother will have been going out of his mind with worry for the last few hours and by now my mother will have joined him.' She paused. 'I would hate to think they should be put through that simply because you wanted to irritate your cousin.'

He glanced up sharply then. Her probing had evidently hit some tender spot. 'They are the only people who will worry about you? What about your father?'

She shrugged. 'My father is of the absentee variety. His only purpose in my mother's life was to provide the means to motherhood. She's a card-carrying feminist of the old school, you see. And a pioneer of single-parenthood. She's written books about it.'

'I wouldn't have thought the subject was so difficult that anyone would need to buy a book to discover how it was done,' he replied drily.

Well, fancy that. The man had a sense of humour.

'They are not do-it-yourself manuals,' she informed him. 'More in the line of philosophical commentary.'

'You mean she felt the need to justify her actions?'

Straight to the point and no messing. She liked that, and found it rather difficult to stop herself from smiling at his bluntness. 'Quite possibly,' she said. 'Maybe when this is over you should ask her.'

Her smile dared him. 'Maybe I will,' he said. 'Do you mind? Not having a father?'

He was getting rather close to her own tenderest spot. 'Do you?' she asked, and knew the answer even before the words were out of her mouth.

His look was thoughtful, and she thought perhaps she had given away rather more than she should have. Act dumb, Rosie, she reminded herself. Act dumb. But he let it go. 'Why did you come here?'

'To Ras al Hajar?' she asked. 'I thought you had that all worked out.'

'You could have gone to the West Indies for winter sun and fun.'

'Yes, I could. But my brother invited me here. It's a while since I've seen him.'

'Abdullah invited you here. Abdullah laid on his personal 747 to bring you here—'

'No,' she said. 'That was for you.' His gaze was unblinking. 'Surely? I mean, he wouldn't...'

'He wouldn't cross the road to shake my hand. I merely took advantage of a flight that had already been arranged. There seemed little to be gained by compounding the extravagance for a point of principle.'

'Oh.' Hassan was right. She should have accepted a long-standing invitation to visit Barbados.

'My cousin is planning to use you to further his political ambitions, Miss Fenton. What I want to know is whether you're an unwitting pawn, or whether you've come here specifically to help him.'

'Help him?' Apparently there was a lot more to this than embarrassing his cousin. 'I think you're overestimating my influence, Your Highness.' The flicker of irritation that crossed his face at her disobedience in insisting on the title was oddly pleasing.

'No, Miss Fenton. If anything I underestimated you. And I have asked you not to call me Your Highness. The title is Abdullah's. For the moment.'

So close to the throne, but never aspiring to it. Maybe. She wondered how Hassan had felt when he was passed over for a younger half-brother. Disinherited after being brought up as a favourite grandson. How old would he have been? Twenty? Twenty-one? There was certainly a battle for power going on here, but she was beginning to think that whoever came out on top it wasn't likely to be young Faisal.

Rose propped her elbows on the table and nibbled at another almond. 'I'll do a deal with you. If you don't call me Miss Fenton in that particularly irritating tone of voice again, I won't call you Your Highness. What do you say?'

CHAPTER FOUR

HASSAN almost laughed aloud. Almost. Rose Fenton was doing a pretty good job of making 'Your Highness' sound more like an insult than anything he could manage, and he doubted it was by chance.

'Am I allowed to call you Miss Fenton in any other tone of voice?' he enquired, as politely as dignity allowed. He just knew she would take advantage of any sign of weakness.

'Better stick to Rose,' she advised. 'It'd be safer. Now, about my mother—'

Oh, no. He wasn't getting involved in a cosy chat about her mother. 'I deeply regret the anxiety your disappearance will cause her. I sincerely wish I could allow you to call her and put her mind at rest.'

'In what way "at rest"?' She didn't feel the need to restrain her feelings, he realised as she laughed mirthlessly. A broad gesture took in her surroundings. 'What exactly would I tell her?'

'That you are in no danger.'

'That's for me to decide, Your Highness, and I have to tell you that the jury's still out.' Her eyes were dark, her look direct, and they told him that she wasn't interested in his fake platitudes. That his 'regret' cut no ice with her. 'And for your information I don't think my mother would be very impressed either.'

Not if she was anything like her daughter. 'You're close?' he asked.

Rose looked startled by that. 'Yes,' she said. 'I suppose so.' Not that close, he suspected. Two strong and independent-minded women would grate uncomfortably against one another. As if she realised that she wasn't being convincing, she added, 'She's very protective.'

'Good. She'll be far more useful to my cause if she's thoroughly roused.'

She let out a sharp, explosive little breath that betrayed her outrage at being tricked like that. 'What *is* your cause?' she demanded. 'What's so special that you think you've the right to do this?' He'd been waiting for the question, but he was sure she wouldn't expect a straight answer. He wasn't about to give her a crooked one, so he took a date from the dish, bit into the sweet flesh without answering her. She gave him a we'll-get-back-to-that-one look and changed tack. 'What'll you do if my mother decides to keep a low profile and leave all the fuss to the Foreign Office? I'm sure Tim will advise her to do that.'

'The more I see of you...' He checked himself. 'The more I *hear* of you, Rose, the more confident I become that she will do exactly what she wants. Almost certainly the opposite of any advice she is given.'

Was that a compliment? Rose couldn't be sure.

'And if she disappoints you? Won't all this have been a waste a time? I assume embarrassing Abdullah is the prime motive for my abduction?'

'Do you?'

She didn't, not for a minute. There was far more to

this than simply irritating Abdullah. But with luck she could provoke him into revealing his purpose.

Hassan sat back and watched her. He had anticipated that she would have done her homework, would quickly catch on to the tension underlying the deceptively peaceful surface of Ras al Hajar. He was right.

'What other reason could there be?' she asked, in a voice far too innocent.

To stop her being used by Abdullah, to distract him, to give Partridge time to get Faisal home. But now he had Rose Fenton sitting beside him, her character as fiery as her hair, he could think of any number of reasons for keeping her. All of them personal.

'Embarrassing Abdullah is not my prime motive. Just a happy side effect. Which is why I won't be leaving the public relations aspect to him.' He checked his watch. 'We're three hours ahead of London. There's plenty of time for your disappearance to make the mid-evening news.'

Rose, scarcely able to believe the arrogance of the man, managed to resist looking at her own wristwatch. 'Are you telling me you've issued a press release?'

'Not yet.' And he smiled. Smiled! 'Not until the last minute. I don't want to give your Foreign Office time to check the facts and hear Abdullah's pressing reasons for keeping the story under wraps. You'll be one of those ''word is just coming in'' stories. I'm sure you can fill in the gaps without my assistance.'

'Yes.' She could fill them in, all right. Just as she could imagine the buzz of adrenalin in the newsroom as the story broke while they were on air. Run with it? Don't run with it? Time it right and they wouldn't have a choice. Not unless they were prepared to allow some other network to grab a scoop on one of their own reporters being kidnapped. After all, Gordon knew where she was, had implied there was something brewing. He'd phone her mother first to warn her, if he could, check if she'd heard anything, but it was too big a story to ignore. 'How will you send it?'

Hassan smiled again at her apparently casual question. 'Not from here.'

No. She shrugged. 'Oh, well, it was worth a try.' If he thought she hoped to get to whatever communication equipment he had tucked away and yell for help, he would be less inclined to wonder if she had any of her own. 'Why don't you tell me what this is all about?' she asked. 'You seem to think I have some influence. I might be able to help.'

'You're hoping for a scoop?' That appeared to amuse him. 'Isn't *being* the story sufficient for you?'

'It's getting to be a rather dangerous habit.'

'There's no danger here,' he promised. Laughter did something wonderful to the lean features of his face and his voice was velvet-soft. 'Just a little celebrity. It should do wonders for your status. You'll be able to name your price when you negotiate your next contract.'

'I'm not in the entertainment business.'

'Oh, come on, Rose. We both know that news is very big business. Twenty-four-hour-a-day television. And if you can put a pretty woman in the front line it adds a certain frisson of excitement, a touch of glamour. Believe me, the world will be glued to its television sets worrying about the brave and lovely Rose Fenton.

Newsmen will be storming the embassy door for visas and poor Abdullah will have to let them come or risk being pilloried in the world's press. You news persons take these things so personally.'

His amusement angered her like nothing else. How dared he be amused? How dared he sit there, enjoying his coffee, while out there her family would be going out of their minds with worry? How dared he treat her like one of his namby-pamby bimbos with nothing on her mind but where the next diamond was coming from?

She was a journalist, a serious journalist, and if she and her family were being put through the grinder for his amusement she wanted the whole story. She was entitled to that. 'I've a right to know why I'm here.'

'You know why you're here. You're in Ras al Hajar to relax, recuperate. You can do that up here near the mountains far more pleasantly than you can in town. It's cooler, the atmosphere is drier. You can ride, swim in the stream, sunbathe. The food is good, the hospitality legendary.' He offered her an intricately wrought silver dish. 'You should try one of these dates. They're really good.'

She stood up abruptly, dashing the dish from his hand so that the fruit flew everywhere. 'Stuff your dates,' she said, and stormed out of the tent and into the night.

It was a grand gesture, but an empty one. Outside there was nothing but darkness and the desert. But Rose wasn't about to turn around and go back inside, face his further amusement at her total loss of self-control. She should be probing, questioning, keeping her mind completely detached from what was happening. But she couldn't. It was just too personal.

Aware that Hassan's men, gathered about a campfire a little distance from the tent, had stopped talking and had turned to see what she would do, she spun on her heel and headed in the direction of the Land Rover. She tried the door. It was unlocked.

Her scarf slipped back from her hair as she pulled herself up into the driving seat and she shivered a little. Hassan was right; it was cooler at the camp. Up here, he'd said. They must be near the mountains at the border. She tried to picture the map, but they were miles off the road and she had no idea which way the road was. North. She was sure it would be north. If she headed for the North Star she would eventually reach the coast. Maybe.

Not that anyone had left the keys conveniently in the ignition. Life wasn't that simple. Oh, well. She yanked out the wires and touched them together. The engine roared into life, startling her almost as much as the men, who until that moment had been idly watching her, grinning stupidly in the firelight.

They leapt up, falling over themselves to get to her. They would have been about twenty seconds too late. Hassan was not so slow. As she slammed the Land Rover into reverse he opened the door and, without bothering to ask what she thought she was doing, he lifted her bodily from the seat and the vehicle stalled. Then he tucked her beneath his arm and headed back towards the tent.

This time she did yell. She yelled and she screamed and would have punched him too, but her arms were trapped so all she could do was flail her hands uselessly at his body. He didn't appear to notice.

It wasn't that she'd expected to get away. In fact she wasn't at all sure she wanted to be racing over unknown terrain in the darkness. But she *was* sure that this was the most humiliating thing ever to happen to her. The fact that she'd brought it on herself did nothing to help.

'Let me go!' she demanded, using both hands in her attempt to lever his arm from around her waist.

'And if I did? Where would you run to?' He stood her up on the rug in the middle of the spilled dates, catching her wrists so that she couldn't strike out at him. 'Stop it. Stop acting like a silly girl and tell me what you planned to do.' She had no plan. He knew that as well as she did. But he wasn't leaving it. 'Come on, don't be coy, Miss Fenton, it's not your style to keep your thoughts to yourself. You've proved unexpectedly useful when it comes to hot-wiring a Land Rover. I applaud your spirit. But what next? Where were you going?' She didn't answer, but was pleased to note that he was no longer laughing. 'What's this? You have nothing to say? You're not normally so slow with a pithy response.'

Her response to this was both pithy and to the point. Whether he was happy with it was debatable, since his brows rose like a high-speed elevator.

'My interest is purely practical, Miss Fenton.' So, they were back to the sarcastic 'Miss Fenton'. 'I'd like to know what you have in mind so that in the unlikely event that you get beyond the perimeter of the camp there's some chance we'll find you before the sun bleaches your bones—'

'All right! You've made your point. I'm an idiot, but what about you, Hassan?' She'd stopped bothering to struggle. She was strong, but he was more than a match for her. 'How can you do this?' She stared at him. 'You're an educated man. You know that this is wrong, that even here, where you're apparently a real old-fashioned warlord you've no right to do this.'

'Do what?' He yanked her towards him so that his face was close enough for her to see the muscle working in his face, for her to see the blaze of anger heating up the steely grey of his eyes. 'What exactly do you think I'm going to do to you?'

Oh, heck, she'd done it now. She'd really done it, but she wasn't going down without a fight. 'What exactly do you *think* I think, Your-Seriously-High-and-Mightiness?' Sarcasm, after all, was a game for two. 'You've already kidnapped me,' she said, flinging the words at him. 'You're keeping me here against my will—' Far worse, he'd made her lose control. Even when Michael had died, even when she'd been doing reports live to camera with rockets landing all around her and the crew, she'd never broken down and completely lost it the way she had just then. There were tears stinging the back of her lids. Tears of pure rage and utter frustration. 'You've got an imagination. Put yourself in my shoes and use it!'

Somehow his hands, instead of grasping her wrists, were at her back, gentling her. And her face was pressed against his heart. There was a comfort in the steady beat beneath her cheek, comfort in the warmth of his arms about her as she sobbed into the blackness of his robes. It was so long since she'd cried. Five years. Nearly six. Longer since she'd let a man hold her close while she exposed her emotions, provoked a caring response.

Not that Hassan cared. Not really. He was just better at dealing with hysterics that most men of her acquaintance. If he went in for this sort of thing on a regular basis he probably got a lot of practice. It was a thought to tense the steel in her backbone and she pushed away from him, lifted her head, forced a smile to her lips.

'I'm sorry about that. Losing control is so...' She sniffed a little, palmed away a tear. 'So messy. Not my kind of thing at all. You'd better put it down to the kind of day I'm having. If you'll excuse me, I'll just go and lie down in a darkened...er...room for a while.' She turned, and was halfway to the bedroom when he said her name.

'Rose.' She didn't like her name very much. She'd shortened it from Rosemary, which she loathed. But Hassan said it as if it was the most beautiful word in the entire world. She stopped, could do nothing else, and waited with her back to him. 'Promise me that you won't do anything like that again.' Or what? She turned. His expression was no longer angry. She couldn't tell what he was feeling. Well, that was fine. She was totally confused herself. 'Please.'

She suspected that asking, rather than telling, did not come easily to him. 'I can't do that, Hassan,' she said, almost with regret. 'If I can escape, I will.'

'You're making this a lot more difficult than it has to be.'

She shrugged. If he was uncomfortable with the role he'd chosen, he would have to live with it. 'You could always let me go.' Then, maybe, she would stay of her own accord. It wasn't the company she objected to, just the manner of it.

'I was hoping I might persuade you to think of yourself as my guest. This way you force me to make you my prisoner.'

'You invite a guest,' Rose said, ridiculously disappointed. 'You could have invited me.'

'You'd have come?'

Maybe. Probably. In a heartbeat. But she couldn't tell him that. Not now. And they both knew that as a guest her presence wouldn't serve his purpose. Instead she extended her wrists to him, holding them close together, palm upward, offering them as if for the handcuffs. 'Perhaps it's time we both recognise the truth of the situation.'

For a moment he stared at her, his face livid in the flaring lamplight. Then he stepped up to her, took her proffered wrists and, holding them easily in one hand, pulled free the scarf that now trailed untidily from her neck. Without a word, he bound her wrists, wrapping the scarf around them once, twice, three times, in a purely symbolic gesture but one that left her in absolutely no doubt of the situation. As if to drive home the point, he caught the loose ends, wrapped them swiftly about his fist and yanked her towards him.

Her protest evaporated in a quick gasp as he caught her shoulders and pulled her hard against his body, so that her head had nowhere to go but backwards, leaving her vulnerable, exposed.

'Is this what you want?' She didn't believe it. She didn't believe he was going to do this. He wouldn't.

Even as she opened her mouth to warn him that he was making a big mistake, he did.

His lips were hard, demanding, punishing her for daring to defy him, for making him do this. But even while her head was telling her to fight, to kick, bite, make him pay with all the limited means at her disposal, feminine instinct kicked in with a ferocity that took away what little breath she had.

This man is strong, it told her. This man would protect her against the worst the world could throw at her, he would give her strong children and lay down his life to defend them.

It was primitive, the female picking out the strongest male in the group for her mate. It was elemental and savage. But beneath the insistent, provoking heat of his mouth, his tongue, Rose knew that in some way she didn't quite understand she had won.

And with that knowledge she melted, dissolved, and for long, blissful seconds she surrendered herself and gave him back everything she had, meeting the marauding silk of his tongue with all the siren sweetness at her command. Oh, yes, she wanted this. She wanted him. In more than five years she had never been tempted, but from the moment he had turned to look at her as he boarded Abdullah's 747 she'd known; this was the moment she had been waiting for.

Then, when she was quite boneless in his arms, his to take with a word, Hassan released her without warning, so that she swayed and staggered.

For a moment he continued to stare at her, as if he could not quite believe what he had done. Then he stepped back. 'I, too, hate to lose control,' he said, his face a mask of restraint. 'Now I believe we are quite even.' And with that he spun on his heel and walked from the tent.

Rose could scarcely catch her breath, could scarcely stand, and she clutched at the chair-back, at the table, staring at the pale silk that Hassan had used to bind her wrists.

She was still trembling, not with rage, but with un-fulfilled longings. She pulled her hands free, flung the scarf to the floor and raced to the opening of the tent, but Hassan had disappeared into the night. There was just a long-legged hunting dog stretched out across the entrance, and a little way off stood an armed man who, at her fierce glance, bowed respectfully.

No more silly grins, she noticed. Well, that was something. She was tempted to test her guard's purpose, but there seemed little point. She had pressed the point and she had got her answer, more answer than she was quite comfortable with. Now she would have to live with it.

She heard the Land Rover starting up, moving off at speed. Hassan, having been delayed by the need to put her firmly in her place, was presumably racing off to alert the world's media to her disappearance.

She lifted her chin a little and told herself she was glad to see him go. Yet the camp felt ridiculously empty without him, and, as if sensing her loneliness, the dog stood up and pushed a nose up against her hand. She stroked his narrow silky head on automatic, then turned away and surveyed her prison.

She checked at the mess of dates on the priceless rug and stooped to pick them up. Then she realised what she was doing and, angry with herself, stopped, backed off and skirted them as she retreated to the refuge of the bedroom. The dog followed her and lay at the foot of the bed.

Waiting, no doubt, for the return of his master, Rose thought. Well, tough. There was only one bed. It was a big bed, but she was there first and she wasn't in the mood to share. A small voice warned her that after the way she had kissed Hassan she could scarcely expect a choice. An even smaller voice suggested that she would be fooling herself if she pretended she wanted one.

She put her hand to her mouth. What on earth had she done? She wasn't in the habit of jumping into bed with just any man who abducted her. Just any man, full stop. She was too busy these days for the falling in love stuff. Been there, done that. Crossed it off the list.

Hassan certainly knew how to re-ignite a girl's interest.

Rose suspected that Hassan could ignite just about anything he chose to fix with eyes that had heated her from frost to meltdown faster than she could say it. She'd recognised him for what he was the moment she had set eyes on him. A very dangerous man.

She kicked off her shoes and flung herself on the bed. The telephone dug into her thigh.

Hassan put his foot hard on the throttle and drove from the camp as if the hounds of hell were after him. Did she know? Did she understand what she'd done? He was gripping the wheel so hard that even in the darkness the bones showed white through his skin.

Why did she have to be like that? It was hard enough

that she was beautiful. But he could resist beautiful. He'd resisted the charms of any number of beautiful women who would have been happy to be held captive in his desert encampment. Maybe that was the difference. Rose Fenton was wilful, strong. She fought him.

She scorned him for what he'd done and then held out her hands to him and dared him to do his worst. In that moment she'd jarred loose the civilised veneer he wore so casually over his desert heritage and laid him bare to the bone, stripped him back to the man his grandfather had been in his youth, a desert warrior who had fought for and taken whatever he wanted, whether it was land, or horses, or a woman.

He'd never had to do that and yet he hadn't thought twice about it. He'd made his plans, summoned the men who would do whatever he asked of them and he'd taken Rose Fenton from under the very nose of her brother.

He'd thought it would be difficult. She had a reputation for toughness and he'd thought she would fight him. It hadn't been like that. Her toughness had made it easier. She hadn't been afraid. She'd been cool, curious. She wanted the story. Or she had until her nerves momentarily let her down and she bolted.

Even then she'd defied him, mocked him, urged him to do his worst and, by heaven, he had come close. He'd bound her wrists as if she was some prize he'd captured in a raiding party, to do with as he willed. He'd bound her wrists and kissed her and had been a heartbeat from taking it all.

But even then she'd won. Not by fighting him. There had been no struggle for honour, nothing to heat his blood and drive him over the edge. She'd been cleverer than that. Cooler than he'd given her credit for. She'd called his bluff and kissed him right back, hot and sweet. Lava on snow.

It was just as well she had no idea it wasn't a bluff or one of them would have been in deep trouble.

He had a feeling it would have been him. If Partridge didn't find Faisal soon, it still might be.

Rose retrieved the telephone from her pocket and for once in her life found it hard to know what to do best. She knew she should contact someone, but who?

Not Tim. She wasn't involving him. Caught like some piggy in the middle between two feuding princes, he could only get crushed.

Gordon, then. Yes, Gordon. She really should call her news editor. Except he would be getting a press release courtesy of Hassan at any moment. All she could add was the name of her abductor, and she wasn't quite ready for that. That would mean choosing sides, and although her head suggested that Abdullah, as Regent, as her brother's employer, deserved her loyalty, her heart just wasn't in it. Tim's warning had been unnecessary; she'd quickly seen for herself that Abdullah intended to use her.

Wasn't that what Hassan was doing?

Maybe. But at least he was frank about it. And she wasn't prepared to hold the fact that Hassan could kiss a woman senseless against him. It didn't *necessarily* mean he was bad. The odds were against it, but she was prepared to give him a chance. Several chances, even.

So what had happened to the totally impartial journalist?

She was on hold. Waiting for the facts, waiting for the truth to emerge. And, since she had no option but stick around, she'd hold the call to the office until she had a story to file. The real story. No sense in wasting the battery after all.

Her mother. She could at least privately assuage Hassan's conscience and reassure her mother. Not that he would know about it, of course. She punched in the number. It was engaged and remained engaged, although she tried again every few minutes until it became quite obvious that she was too late; her mother had heard the news, presumably from Tim, and was already in full vent. And her mother understood the power of the press. Forget the Foreign Office; her first call would be to Gordon. Lucky Hassan.

She switched off, closed the phone and looked about her. She'd been fortunate so far that he hadn't thought to search her. Until that kiss she'd assumed he was being a gentleman. It seemed more likely that the women he knew who wore such traditional garments didn't carry mobile phones.

She could not rely on her luck holding out for ever, however. She needed a secure hiding place for her one link with the outside world. A link she might yet have a desperate need for. And she might not have much time.

There was a new box of tissues on the dressing table. She ripped open the top, removed some of the tissues to make a space, then pushed the palm-sized phone to the bottom of the box, tidied it, pulled a tissue up so that it looked as if she'd been using them.

She was left with a pile of tissues which she wadded extravagantly and used with the cleanser provided by her thoughtful host to remove her make-up. Then tossed them untidily beside the box to prove what she'd done with them.

She yawned. Nerves, tension, exhaustion, combining suddenly in a need for sleep. Yet the thought of stripping to her underwear was slightly unnerving. Except surely any man who had gone to such lengths to provide her with her favourite cosmetics wouldn't have overlooked the fact that she'd need a change of clothes? She pulled back the bedcover. No, he hadn't forgotten.

She picked up the nightdress that had been neatly folded and left beneath the cover for her, and shook it out. It was...it was... She found herself biting back a grin. It was such a thoroughly *reassuring* garment. So completely *respectable*. It was the kind of nightgown that a Victorian spinster would feel safe in. No man with ravishment on his mind would choose anything like it, not unless he planned to fight his way through yards and yards of winceyette and cotton lace. Presumably that *was* the point he was trying to make. The dog had lifted his head at her stifled giggle and now thumped his tail hopefully.

'All right,' she said. 'So he's not all bad.' She held up the nightgown. 'But I'd like to know where on earth he found something like this. In his grandmother's attic, do you suppose?' It would have to have been his Scottish grandmother's attic. It was just the thing for a cold Highland night. She shivered. Just the thing for a cold desert night, too.

She slipped out of the silk two-piece that she'd chosen with such care, with such hopes of impressing the interesting Mr Partridge and his master. What a waste of time that had been. Simon Partridge wasn't actually in the country and Hassan would have abducted her even if she'd been wearing a pair of combats.

Although, on second thoughts, she doubted that combats would have drawn the same startled glance when she'd joined him for dinner. Unfortunately, she couldn't decide whether that was a good thing or not. Did she want to be that noticeable? She pulled a face as she picked up a hairbrush. Cursed with hair the colour of a Technicolor sunset, how could she be anything else?

When she finally climbed into the vast bed, settling the folds of the voluminous nightgown about her, she decided that her mother would have approved of it. It was draughtproof, oozed comfort, and what it lacked in length it more than made up for in width.

Her last thought before falling asleep was to wonder whether Hassan had raided the same wardrobe for her day-wear.

Would she wake up to find a good tweed skirt laid out for her? A cashmere twinset in a nice, sensible heather mixture? A pair of solid knickers with a double-stitched gusset and the kind of stout elastic that discouraged wandering hands...

The idea should have been reassuring. Somehow it wasn't.

Hassan sat beside the bed for a long time just watching her. How could a woman who had created such havoc sleep so peacefully? It was tempting to wake her, disturb her, except that he suspected he would be the one made to suffer.

She was so lovely, her skin so pale against the bright copper of her hair. She hadn't given him an inch all evening and even in sleep she had the power to disturb him more than any woman he'd known.

It wasn't a comfortable feeling. He didn't like it. But he suspected that when she went away it would be even worse.

CHAPTER FIVE

ROSE stirred. She felt warm and wonderfully comfortable and snuggled further beneath the covers, untroubled by any inclination to leap out of bed and get on with life. This was nice. She shifted slightly. The warm weight against her back shifted too, moulding itself snugly against the curve of her spine. That was nice too. It had taken her so long to get used to waking alone.

Rose froze, slowly opened her eyes, all senses on full alert.

She was not alone. *Not alone.*

The sunlight was being filtered softly through the black goathair of Hassan's tent. Her gaze flickered over the antique campaign chest, standing open in the corner, with her make-up scattered on the inner lid. Over the soft sheen of a priceless carpet. Over the heavy silk of her *shalwar kameez*, neatly folded on a camel stool next to the bed. And the weight at her back was a solid reality, definitely not a figment of some dream she was still waking from.

The fuzzy feeling of comfort rapidly evaporated as the events of the previous evening flooded back with vivid and terrible clarity. What was a girl to do? Should she turn and let her captor take her in his arms and finish what they had started last night? Or should she opt for outrage?

She quickly opted for outrage before she could weaken, erupting from the covers in a flurry of indignation. Her companion erupted too, leaping to his paws and barking excitedly.

It was the dog. Just the dog.

She fell back against the pillow and allowed her heart-rate to subside a little. Not Hassan. Relief warred with disappointment. She had definitely been alone too long.

The dog yawned widely, then settled down again with his head laid flat on her stomach. 'So, you get to sleep on the bed, do you?' she said, once she'd regained her breath. 'My mother would have a fit if she could see you.' She stroked his head. 'She doesn't approve of dogs on the bed.' She didn't approve much of husbands either. Only lovers received her seal of approval. It was one of those mother/daughter disagreements that still festered between them, long after the husband was no more.

Something, some movement out of the corner of her eye made her look up. Hassan, attracted no doubt by the noise, had swept the drapes aside.

'You slept well?'

Amazingly well, while he looked as if he'd had a very bad night indeed. But before she could ask her brain to compute a sensible answer they were interrupted.

'I knew it!' A small woman, heavily cloaked and veiled in an *abbeyah*, appeared at his side and, without waiting for an invitation, pushed past. Then, having confirmed her worst suspicions, turned on him. 'For heaven's sake, Hassan!' Outrage, heavily laced with ex-asperation. 'What on earth are you thinking of?'

Was it his wife? Rose hadn't even thought about a wife. It was a long time since she'd blushed, but faced with almost terminal embarrassment she discovered that she still remembered how.

Hassan did not immediately reply, or attempt to defend himself. The woman apparently had no expectation that he would, since she didn't wait, but swept up to the bed. Tossing aside the cloak and veil, she revealed herself as a young and very beautiful woman dressed, beneath the traditional trappings of purdah, in a heavy silk shirt and a beautifully cut skirt that stopped just short of her knee.

'Nadeem al Rashid,' she said, extending a small hand to Rose. 'I apologise unreservedly for my brother's behaviour. His heart is in the right place but, like most men, he has the brains of a donkey. You're coming home with me right now; you'll be safe there until Faisal returns. And in the meantime we can think of some way to explain your disappearance.'

Faisal? Rose's mind clicked into gear. This girl couldn't be more than Hassan's half-sister. That would make her Faisal's full blood sister, and yet she was clearly intent on mopping up Hassan's mess. Direct action seemed to be a family trait.

Rose glanced at him, but he appeared to be avoiding meeting her gaze and she bit down on her lip. It wouldn't do to be grinning too obviously; she'd just sit back and watch the fun as Nadeem turned on him.

'What on earth were you thinking of, Hassan?' She repeated the question, but didn't give him a chance to answer. 'No, don't tell me, I can guess. Have you spoken to Faisal?' Hassan sent her a warning look, which she ignored. 'Well?'

He could see there was no stopping her, so he shrugged and conceded the point. 'I sent Partridge to the States to bring him home but he's slipped his guards and taken off somewhere.'

'How inconsiderate of him,' she said drily. 'I wonder who taught him that trick?'

'I'm handling it,' he said, through gritted teeth. 'Just leave it to me.'

'I don't think so.'

'No one asked what you thought, Nadeem. I want you to leave now. This is my problem and I don't want to get anyone else involved.' He didn't want his sister getting into trouble and Rose found herself unexpectedly in sympathy with him.

'I am involved, idiot. Faisal is my brother, too.'

'If it goes wrong…'

'With you in charge? How can it?' Rose had thought she could do sisterly sarcasm, but this young woman could take the simplest sentence and make it really hurt. 'Take no notice of him,' Nadeem said, returning her attention to Rose. 'I've brought a spare *abbeyah*; no one will see you arrive at my house.' She turned on her brother. 'You've behaved disgracefully, Hassan. Miss Fenton is a guest in our country…' She slipped into Arabic and clearly vilified his character in no uncertain terms.

Rose watched the scene played out before her with a growing desire to laugh. There was something about a powerful man being roundly taken to task by one of his female relations that left her wanting to cheer. Then, over Nadeem's gesticulating arms, her glossy black hair, her gaze finally connected with that of Hassan. It was as if she could read his mind.

'Um, excuse me.' She waved a hand and Nadeem stopped her tirade long to enough to turn and stare at her. 'I hate to interrupt when you're clearly doing a fine job of reading Hassan his character, but do I get a say in this?'

And from behind his sister Hassan's eyes thanked her.

Well, that was great, but she wasn't doing it for him. This was a purely professional decision. The last thing she wanted was to be rescued by Princess Nadeem, no matter how well intentioned her motives. She'd be taken to town and kept out of sight and out of contact. At least here she was in the centre of things. Close to Hassan...where everything was happening.

Nadeem, though, misunderstood, and came and sat down on the bed, took her hand in her own. It was tiny, exquisitely manicured, beautifully painted in hennaed arabesques. She made Rose feel like some ungainly giantess.

'Miss Fenton, I realise that you simply want to go back to your brother's house and resume your holiday, but we have something of a problem. Abdullah is close to seizing the throne and Faisal, stupid boy, has chosen this moment to...well...let's say his timing is a little off.' She spat some words at Hassan that undoubtedly involved the stupidity of men in general and of her brothers in particular. 'The uproar caused by your disappearance will keep Abdullah in check for a few days, and if you'll stay with me until everything is sorted out I am sure Hassan will make sure your sacrifice does not go unrewarded.'

'Unrewarded?' She repeated the word. What was Nadeem saying? She'd get the Ras al Hajar equivalent of the Order of Merit?

'Well, Rose,' he said, softly. He was standing behind his sister and she looked up at him. 'It would seem that you can name your own price. A *lakh* of gold…a rope of pearls—'

'"And Thou Beside me singing in the Wilderness"?' Not honour, then. Just plain old gold, she thought, as she completed his alternative version of the line from *The Rubaiyat of Omar Khayyam*.

'Whatever you wish,' he replied.

That momentary glimpse of the man behind the eyes, a man capable of love, would do to be going on with. '*Can* you sing?'

'Like a nightingale.' *Oh, sure.* 'Or was it a crow?'

'The story, Hassan,' she snapped. 'That's all I want. The story, the whole story and nothing but the story. And I stay here.'

Nadeem looked momentarily startled. 'But you can't—'

'She can and she must.' Hassan, with her co-operation assured, regained mastery of the situation. 'I assure you that Miss Fenton's sacrifice will be no greater than she chooses.'

'Oh, but—'

'Haven't you got a clinic today, Nadeem?'

'This afternoon.' She glanced at her wristwatch. 'Actually, since I'm here, could I ask you about some new incubators?'

'Tell Partridge what you want. He'll sort it out.'

Nadeem certainly knew how to pick her moments, Rose thought as the dark beauty smiled so that her entire face lit up. 'I thank you. The mothers and babies of Ras al Hajar thank you, Hassan. Now, Miss Fenton—'

'Rose, please.'

'Rose.' For a moment she wore a look that suggested she had not finished. Then she made a very feminine gesture of resignation. 'Is there anything I can bring you? Anything you need?'

'Your brother has made every effort to ensure my comfort. Except for clothes.' She plucked at the nightdress. 'This isn't really my style.'

'No?' For a moment Hassan's eyes lingered on the rise and fall of her breasts beneath the solid cloth. 'No,' he repeated, his voice softer. Then he cleared his throat. 'I'm sorry that my choice didn't meet with your approval, but there's a trunk full of stuff in your size. I'm sure you'll find something you like.'

Rose, whose heart was already pounding with quite unnecessary vigour, lurched uncomfortably as he turned to the trunk lid and reached for the box of tissues. The weight would warn him...

'Go *away*, Hassan,' Nadeem said. 'You've no business in here.'

'Rose Fenton is not one of your wilting virgins, Nadeem. If she wants me to leave, she'll say so.' He glanced at her. There was no apparent change in his expression and yet she knew, deep down, he was smiling. 'I guarantee it. But you're right. If you two are going to be sorting through clothes, I'd rather be somewhere else. Will you stay and have breakfast, Nadeem?'

'Just some coffee,' she said, waving him away with an imperious gesture. She waited until he had gone, then checked the outer room before turning back to Rose. 'Look, it doesn't matter what Hassan says. If you don't want to stay here you don't have to. Just say the word and you can leave with me now.'

No. She'd stay and see it through. She had promised Hassan as much. The words might have been in her head, but she knew and so did he.

'No. I'll be fine. Really.'

Nadeem's smile was knowing, and hoping to distract her, hoping to distract herself, Rose asked, 'What's a *lakh* of gold? Some kind of jewellery?'

'A *lakh*?' Nadeem was clearly astonished at her ignorance of something of such importance. 'No. It's a weight. A hundred thousand grams.' *Of gold?* Rose tried to imagine how much that was and failed. Nadeem, however, dismissed it as nothing. 'Don't worry about it. Whether you stay here or come home with me Hassan will still have to pay your brother for carrying you off the way he did.'

'Pay my brother?' She could just imagine Tim's reaction to that. Even Nadeem might learn a thing or two about indignation. If Hassan offered him money for his sister's honour it was quite possible that Tim might break the habit of a lifetime and actually hit him.

But Nadeem was serious. 'Of course he must pay. He has dishonoured you.' She was thoroughly matter-of-fact about it. Did she take it for granted that Hassan had shared her bed? Rose wondered. Or did just being alone with him at his camp count? She thought it wiser not to ask. 'Or maybe your brother will just kill him?' Nadeem suggested.

'Er... I don't think so.' Even indignant, she didn't see Tim offering Hassan much more than a sock on the jaw.

'No?' Nadeem shrugged. 'Of course, he is English. Englishmen are so...phlegmatic. Hassan would certainly kill your brother if the situation were reversed. But if you do not want money or blood there is only one other solution. He will have to marry you. Leave it to me. I will arrange it.'

This was getting further into the realms of fantasy than Rose was prepared to go. 'Surely a man of his age, his wealth...' she was beginning to think like Nadeem, she realised '...must be married already?' And, no matter what his sister said, she wasn't sharing.

'Hassan? Married?' Nadeem laughed. 'He'd have to find someone strong enough to hold onto him first.'

'But if marriages are arranged here...?'

'Hassan is different,' she said. 'Hassan is impossible. With you it would be a matter of honour, so he would have no choice, but he wouldn't consider it under any other circumstances. Believe me, we've tried, but he's travelled too much to accept some good, traditional girl who just wants to stay at home and raise children. It wouldn't be kind to either of them. But then he's too traditional to marry one of those actresses or models he spends time with so publicly when he's in London or Paris or New York. Not that it would last five minutes if he brought her back here.'

'Why?'

'Women need to be born to the life. Our men are possessive and modern women do not care to be possessed. They want what Hassan can give them, but they refuse to give up what they already have.' She smiled. 'I pity them.'

'But you are happy.'

'I work at being happy. I have a kind husband, beautiful children and a worthwhile job in a country I love.' She glanced at Rose. 'Hassan loves it here, too. He couldn't live anywhere else.' Then she sighed. 'He would have been a great Emir,' she said. 'He always had it in him. While Faisal…well, Faisal doesn't understand the sacrifices involved.' She thought about it for a moment. 'Or maybe he does…'

'And Abdullah?'

Nadeem started, as if aware she had been letting her mouth run away with her brain, then she glanced at her watch and gave an unconvincing squeak. 'I don't have a lot of time. Let's look at these clothes. I have the feeling you won't find much to your taste.'

'Well?' Hassan regarded her over the remains of her breakfast. 'What did you find out?'

'Find out?'

'My little sister has a runaway mouth. I'm sure you had no difficulty in prising loose all kinds of information.'

'Nadeem is charming and thoughtful and very helpful.'

'If she made that good an impression she must have been unusually garrulous, even for her.'

'Not at all. She told me very little I didn't already know.'

'It's the "very little" that bothers me.'

'Why? Ensuring that Faisal keeps his throne is hardly something to be ashamed of. I had assumed you were planning on seizing it yourself.' If she'd hoped to provoke a reaction, she failed. 'And I'm not going to be telling anyone what you're doing, am I?' She smiled. Not yet, anyway. 'Actually, her main concern seemed to be that you would have to pay my brother dearly for dishonouring me.'

She was teasing him, Hassan decided. Amusing herself at his expense. Well, that was fine. Whatever kept her happy. 'Whatever you think is appropriate,' he said dismissively. A *lakh* of gold would be cheap enough for her co-operation. And she was co-operating. Or very clever. 'Although having met you I begin to doubt that either you or your brother would take so much as a *tula* of my gold.' That at least was the truth. He would stake his life that she was not in Abdullah's pocket. And his heart rejoiced.

'Maybe not, but that leaves you with a problem.' He waited, content to let her have her fun. It was a long time since anyone had amused him half so much. 'According to Nadeem, the only alternatives to a cash settlement would appear to be death or dishonour, and since Tim would die himself rather than kill anyone...' She paused. 'Even you...' He laughed. 'She's decided that marriage is the only answer.'

Rose watched as his hand, carrying a cup to his lips, paused briefly. 'She may be right,' he said. Then he drank his coffee, returned the cup to the saucer and rose to his feet. 'I see that you are wearing jodhpurs. Is that a hint that you would like to ride this morning?'

Well, Rose, she thought. That didn't go quite the way you planned, girl. Not at all. It would certainly teach her not to try being clever before lunchtime. And she discovered she couldn't quite meet the challenge of his gaze. Not yet. But, confronted at eye-level with the ornate *khanjar* he wore at his waist, she realised that he was still waiting for her answer.

Did she want to ride with Hassan? Was that why she'd insisted on wearing the jodhpurs in the face of Nadeem's protest? She was suddenly very confused. It was a long time since she'd ridden a horse alongside the man she loved. A long time since she'd done anything. Even been tempted. But the jodhpurs had seemed so familiar, so comforting...

Still avoiding his eyes, she stretched out her legs. 'They were the only trousers we could find,' she said evasively. 'Oddly, I have this aversion to wearing long silk frocks during the hours of daylight. Even ones with designer labels.'

The underwear had been something else, though. She had not the slightest objection to silk next to the skin. But that was as far as she was prepared to go. Hence the man's shirt and an old pair of jodhpurs she'd raided from Hassan's drawer chest, while Nadeem had looked on, torn between horror and amusement, covering her face with her exquisitely painted hands to hide her giggles.

The shirt was loose and she'd had to cinch in the waist of the jodhpurs with a belt, but they were comfortable. She rubbed her palms over cloth worn soft with use and finally looked up.

'Were they yours?'

He hesitated. 'Probably. I don't remember.' He looked distinctly uncomfortable with the idea of her wearing his clothes, she thought, although it must have been years since he'd worn them. He'd put on a lot of muscle since the jodhpurs had been made for him. 'I would have provided you with your own clothes, but the inference would have been drawn that you had left of your own choice.'

'You brought my boots.' A pair of stout, cross-laced ankle boots that she'd worn with the long woollen skirt she'd travelled in. She'd had no reason to wear them since she arrived and she wouldn't have noticed if they'd been missing for days.

He shrugged. 'The ground out here is rough.'

'And it would be a touch embarrassing if you had to rush me to hospital with a broken ankle.'

He smiled at her apparent naivety. 'Don't be silly. I'd just say I found you like that. You wouldn't betray me, would you, Rose? You'd think of the story and keep your mouth shut.'

The man was insufferable. Right. But insufferable. She abandoned any hope of bettering him and returned to the subject of her clothes. 'Of course, if Khalil had given you all my clothes he would probably have ended up in jail as a conspirator. I don't imagine Abdullah would be very gentle with him.'

'Khalil?'

'My brother's servant. Someone must have passed on information about what make-up I use. And shampoo.

That's a neat shower, by the way.' A small tank had been filled with water and the early sun had heated it to a pleasant warmth. She finished her coffee. 'And who else would have been able to fix the Range Rover without attracting attention? Khalil washes it as often as his face.'

'So,' he said, neither confirming nor denying her musings. 'Do you want to ride?'

'It's one of the promised attractions.'

'*Can* you ride?'

'Yes,' she said, rising to her feet, increasingly uncomfortable as the focus of Hassan's undiluted attention.

'To stay on one of my horses you'll need more than a passing acquaintance with a mild-mannered pony from some genteel riding school for young ladies.'

'I don't doubt it, but I had a good teacher. You aren't worried that I'll be spotted?' she asked, rapidly changing the subject. 'If they use search helicopters?' She rubbed her hand over her hair. 'I'm pretty hard to miss.'

'You do have a way of making your presence felt,' he agreed, with a wry smile. 'But your hair is not a problem. With the right clothes, you'll be as good as invisible. Wait here.'

He returned a few minutes later with a red and white checked *keffiyeh* which he handed to her. She flicked it out of the fresh folds and draped it over her head, then stopped. It was a lot bigger than she had expected and she was at something of a loss to know quite how to deal with it. She held the ends out and looked at him helplessly.

For a moment they both remembered the scarf she

had been wearing and what he had done with that. Then
he took a quick breath. 'Here,' he said. 'Like this.'

He swiftly wrapped it about her head and lower face,
folding it, tucking it into place, his fingers skimming
her cheeks but never quite making contact. Even so, her
stomach clenched at his closeness, at the almost-touch
that raised the down on her face, raised gooseflesh everywhere.

'There. All done.'

'Thank you,' she said, her voice little more than a
whisper from her dry mouth.

'No, thank *you*, Rose. For understanding about
Nadeem. If Abdullah found out...'

'Yeah. Well. I won't get a scoop hiding out in
Nadeem's back parlour, will I?'

Again there was the smile that did nothing to the
muscles of his face, just lit some place behind his eyes.
Then he held out a gold-trimmed camel-hair cloak he'd
been carrying over his arm.

She turned quickly and slipped her arms through the
wide openings and let it hang about her. It was loose
and feather-light and billowed softly about her in the
fresh breeze coming off the mountains and into the tent.

'You look almost like a Bedouin,' he said, wrapping
his own black headcloth around his face.

Rose stroked her chin over the cloth. 'But for the
beard.' She put her head to one side. 'But then you
don't wear a beard, do you, Hassan? Why is that?'

'You ask too many questions,' he said, and with his
hand at her back he eased her through the opening and
into the bright morning sunlight.

'It's what I do. But you're miserly with your answers.'

His response was to direct her to the waiting horses. One was a glorious black stallion, exactly like the one she had taunted him with the previous night. She wondered if it had been chosen deliberately, then decided that her wits were wandering.

The other mount was a smaller, but very beautiful chestnut. 'What's his name?' she asked, as she stroked the animal's neck.

'Iram.'

'Iram indeed is gone with all his Rose...' The line ran through her head and she wondered if he was telling her the truth, or simply testing her to see if she knew more than one line from *The Rubaiyat*. She whispered the name and the horse flicked his ears, lifted his fine head. The truth, then. Or maybe a bit of both. 'How appropriate.'

'I thought so. You know the verse by heart?'

'I was made to learn it at school as a punishment for some misdemeanour... I can't remember what.'

'But you remember the verse.'

'I didn't consider it a punishment. And I never forget anything I love.' She gathered the reins and Hassan linked his hands for her, throwing her up into the saddle before adjusting the stirrups. It was a while since she had been on a horse but, held at the head by the groom, he seemed quiet enough as she continued to stroke his neck.

Hassan mounted, glanced at her, then, apparently satisfied with what he saw, he nodded. The grooms stepped back and the horses leapt forward.

For a moment Rose thought her arms had been yanked out of their sockets and was grateful that Hassan was so far ahead he didn't witness her unseemly struggle with the deceptively docile beast she had been mounted on.

By the time he brought his mount to a halt and turned, rearing, to see what had happened to her, she was in control and flying, sweeping past him in a blur of movement. He thundered after her, passed her and led the way, his black cloak billowing and flying in the wind. It was wonderful, exciting, terrifying all at once, and when he finally came to a halt on the bluff of a hill she was laughing and breathless and trembling from the sheer effort of controlling her mount. Hassan was laughing too.

'You thought he'd be too much for me, didn't you?'

'He very nearly was, but you're an excellent horse-woman.'

She laughed. 'It's just as well. But it's been a while.'

Hassan threw a long leg over the saddle, dismounted, gathered the reins. 'Who taught you?'

'A friend.'

He turned to look at her. 'A man, I think. You ride like a man.'

Rose was keenly aware of his level, penetrating gaze fixed upon her. 'Yes, a man. He bred horses. Beautiful horses.' She stroked the neck of the animal beneath her. The creak, the scent of leather and hot horseflesh brought it all flooding back. 'He was my husband.'

There was a momentary pause while he digested this information. 'Was?' he enquired softly, when she volunteered nothing more. 'You're divorced?'

'No, he died.' There was a moment of silence and she could see him trying to decide whether to ask the question. 'It wasn't a riding accident.' If it had been a riding accident she could never have got on a horse again. 'He had something wrong with his heart. He knew but he didn't tell me.' She hadn't talked about it in more than five years. Had just got on with her life. Tried not to think about it. She took her feet from the stirrups and slid to the ground. 'One day it just stopped. And he died.'

Hassan joined her and, leading the two horses, began to walk them. 'I'm sorry, Rose. I had no idea.'

'It was a long time ago.'

She sensed him glance at her. 'Not that long. You're a young woman.'

'It's been almost six years.' She scarcely saw the landscape that stretched before her. She was seeing the life they might have had. Two children by now, with ponies of their own. Michael had asked her if she wanted children, would have given them to her, but she had resisted the idea. She was young and had wanted all his attention. And there hadn't seemed any urgency.

Her eyes misted and she stumbled against a rock. Hassan caught her, held her, his hand at her waist.

'You are fortunate that you have your career,' he said. 'Something to fill the emptiness.'

'Do you think a job could do that? That any kind of career would compensate for what I lost? I loved him. He loved me.' Unconditionally. As a woman. She hadn't had to compete for his attention, hadn't had to be better, or prove anything. Just be herself.

He looked down at her, deeply thoughtful. 'Tell me,

did you get your reputation for fearlessness because you were hoping to die, too?'

Her immediate response was anger. How dared he think he could psychoanalyse her? She'd had years of her mother doing that. Nodding sagely when she'd married Michael, as if it had confirmed some theory she was working on for her latest feminist tract. But even as she thought the words she knew she was wrong. Hassan's eyes weren't knowing, but smoky soft with a sympathetic grasp of how she'd suffered.

'Maybe,' she whispered, admitting it for the first time. 'Maybe. For a while.'

'Don't be in too much of a hurry, Rose. Allah will come for you in his own good time.'

'I know.' She managed a smile. 'But it's a lot easier to get a reputation than lose it. Of course I've got a busy mouth, and that gets me into all sorts of bother as well.'

And suddenly he was smiling too. 'I've noticed,' he said drily.

He'd noticed, but his voice, although teasing, had a warmth that brought her crashing back into the present. It was now that mattered. Today. And for just a moment, with his hand at her waist, his eyes hotter than the sun beating down on her back, she thought that he was going to kiss her again. But he didn't. She saw the moment when he took the mental step back from the brink a split second before he let his hand drop to his side and moved on.

Well, he wasn't getting off that easily. She had a story to write and it was time to get down to serious research. 'So,' she said, falling in beside him. 'Why *did* you shave off your beard?'

CHAPTER SIX

HASSAN laughed, enjoying the lightning switch from thoughtful introspection to attack. 'Who said I ever had one? It's not compulsory, you know.' She restricted her response to a perfectly judged raising of eyebrows, reminding him wordlessly that she was not some gullible girl he could string along with just any old line. 'You're like a terrier with a bone,' he complained.

'Compliments don't impress me, Hassan, I've heard them all before. Why?' She pressed for an answer, wanting to get under the skin of the man. Find out what really made him tick.

'Maybe I'm just a natural born rebel.'

'Your bog standard black sheep?' Rose didn't think so, and her quick head-to-toe trawl of his figure suggested as much. 'That's a bit obvious, isn't it?'

'I was twenty-one,' he said. 'It's not an age for subtlety. And when something works, why change it?' He led the way to a low flat rock, hitched the horses to a scrubby tree and invited her to sit, offered her a drink from the flask he carried on his saddle.

She pulled the *keffiyeh* loose and swallowed the cold water gratefully. He followed suit, sitting beside her.

Before them the land fell away in a rocky escarpment to the coastal plain, and in the distance Rose could see the flash of sunlight on a sea so blue that it merged with the sky. It was a stark landscape in which the shadows from boulders and the occasional copse of scrubby trees stretched for ever.

Stark, utterly different from the cool greens of home, and yet she could see the attraction. There was something compelling, timeless about it. It was scoured clean and strangely beautiful.

Hassan loved it, Nadeem had said. She could easily believe it was a place that could carve itself into a man's heart. Or a woman's. She glanced at him, still waiting.

He shrugged, rubbed his hand over his clean-shaven chin. 'My grandfather decided that I wouldn't be able to hold the tribes together,' he said. 'It was a difficult time. There was big money pouring in from the oil and he knew that rival families would use the fact that my father was a foreigner to stir up trouble for me.'

'He had no sons of his own to succeed him?'

'No. Half a dozen daughters, but no sons. I was his oldest grandson, but when it came down to it he did what all rulers have to do and put his country before his heart.'

'When he named Faisal his heir?'

'My mother remarried quite soon after my father died. A political match. She had a couple of daughters; Nadeem is one of them. Then she had Faisal. He has the perfect pedigree to rule.'

'He's still very young.'

'I know, but we all have to grow up. It's his time. I only hope he handles it better than me.'

She felt for him. His pain was buried deep, but it was there. 'It must have been hard for you to accept.' And she'd have been hard pressed to say if it was the journalist or the woman who was speaking.

Hassan picked up a stone, squeezed it as if moulding it between his fingers. 'Yes, it was hard. I had nothing but this.' He palmed the stone for a moment and then he tossed it away. 'Then I had nothing.' Rose remained silent. What could she say? He'd been disinherited because of his parentage. No words would ever change that. He glanced at her. 'What made it harder to bear was the fact that he named Abdullah as Regent Emir to keep his enemies quiet.' Then he threw up a hand in a gesture of acceptance. 'He had no choice; I know that. He was protecting me. If I'd been ten years older he might have defied them and I might have held it all together. But he was dying and he was probably right; I was too young to handle that kind of trouble. Now the only trouble we have is Abdullah and his cronies, with their sticky fingers in the coffers while the people yearn for education, medical care, all the advantages of living in the twenty-first century.'

She thought of the luxurious medical centre she had been shown. Everything new. Like the fancy shopping mall crammed with designer boutiques, the fabulous health club where she had been given an instant honorary membership, it had reeked of privilege. She had suspected a downside, had planned to look for it. Apparently she had been right. Rose wrapped her arms about her knees and, with her chin propped on them, she stared out across the empty landscape. 'No one would blame you for taking it badly,' she said.

'No one did. And no one did a thing to stop me. Disinherited, I shaved off my beard, took to wearing black and behaved very badly indeed. He might have taken away my right to the throne, but my grandfather compensated for the loss in other ways. I had too much money and too little sense and set about proving to the world that my grandfather had made the right decision, while Abdullah and his cohorts stood on the sidelines practically cheering me on, hoping I'd self-destruct. I was immature, spoilt and stupid. I know this because my mother, who would do almost anything rather than travel on a plane, flew to London for the sole purpose of telling me so to my face.'

If she was anything like Nadeem, Rose thought, hiding a smile as she did so, he could have been left in no doubt what she thought of him. 'You didn't let your beard grow back, though. Or adopt a slightly more conservative form of dress. Or even moderate your behaviour much.'

'The rebel coming to heel like a whipped dog? Wouldn't Abdullah have enjoyed that. He'd have spread rumours that I was trying to get myself back into favour, planning to make a bid for the throne, the perfect excuse to move against me and Faisal. No, I've made my bed and I'm content to suffer for it until my brother is safely installed in his rightful place.' He glanced down at her. 'And while my least favourite cousin is kept busy scouring the countryside for you, Rose Fenton, there's still time.'

He nodded towards the coast where, below them, a pair of helicopters had appeared and were quartering the ground in a search pattern. He leaned back on an elbow, showing no obvious sign of concern.

'What'll you do if they come to the camp?'

'Shoot the first man who attempts to enter the women's quarters.'

'The women's quarters! Oh, puh-leeze!'

'What is wrong with that?'

He didn't know? 'Well, for a start, there is only me, and I'm not one of your women.'

'You're under my protection. And one woman or a hundred, what difference does it make?'

She stared at him. 'But to kill someone...'

'I didn't say kill. Just shoot. A bullet through the leg of the bravest is usually sufficient to discourage the rest.' He shrugged. 'They would expect nothing less.' Seeing that she still wasn't convinced, he added, 'They'd do the same to me if the situation were reversed.'

She shuddered. 'But that's so...primitive.'

'You think so?' The grey eyes glittered in the bright sunlight. 'Maybe you're right. The primitive is nearer to the surface than most of us are prepared to admit, Rose, as you came close to discovering at first hand last night.'

She felt sure he wasn't referring to her abduction, planned and carried out with such chilling precision. He was talking about that moment when they had both come close to abandoning any pretence at civilised behaviour, to toppling over the edge.

Of course it had just been the tension. Captor and captive bound together in a precarious, supercharged atmosphere, a cauldron of combustible emotions that had, under pressure, reached an almost inevitable flashpoint...

She looked quickly away. The helicopters had moved

further down the coast. 'I think we'd better go back while I can still move. It's weeks since I've had any serious exercise and I'm going to be as stiff as a board after this.'

'Really?' He stood up and offered her his hand. When, after the briefest hesitation, she took it, he pulled her to her feet. For a moment he continued to grasp her fingers against his palm. 'Don't tell me you've been wasting your time down at the health club?'

'If you've been keeping that close an eye on me, Hassan,' she said sharply, 'you'll know exactly what I've been doing.' An early-morning workout with some light weights to get back the muscle tone she'd lost during weeks of enforced idleness. Not much of a preparation for riding one of Hassan's horses.

He neither confirmed nor denied her accusation. 'Just say the word, Rose, and I'll be happy to give you a rub-down with horse liniment.'

For the briefest of moments she allowed her imagination free rein to dwell on the thought of his hands stroking some warming unguent over her shoulders and back, along the tightening muscles of her legs. She didn't doubt he was capable of making her feel a lot better. But she retrieved her hand, pulled a face and managed a laugh.

'Thanks, Hassan, but I think I'd better just suffer. You're in enough trouble already.'

Enough trouble. How much trouble was enough? How far did a man have to go before he had reached the limit of the trouble he could get into and still find a way out at the end?

Always assuming that he wanted a way out.

Hassan paced impatiently, hanging onto the satellite phone, waiting for Simon Partridge to come on the line. Waited and told himself to face reality.

Rose Fenton was a woman with the world about to fall at her feet. In another week the press would be pleading for her story. Hollywood would probably want to make a film of it and her agent would be holding an auction for the book.

Every time he went near her he made it easier for her. She only had to look at him and he wanted to tell her his deepest secrets, innermost longings, longings that seemed to involve a lifetime spent getting to know her.

Instead he'd offered to rub her down. How crass could one man get? Except that it was all too easy to imagine the warm silk of her skin sliding beneath his hand.

His groan was heartfelt. He needed this to be over. Quickly.

'Come on, Partridge! Where the devil are you!'

Silk skin, silk lips. He stopped, closed his eyes, and for a moment allowed himself to drown in the memory of her warm lips parting for him, the sweet taste of her on his tongue.

He'd intended to keep this strictly impersonal. Keep his distance. It should have been easy. She was a journalist, and he disliked journalists on principle. But from the moment he'd answered the phone and her voice had filled his head he'd been hooked.

He stopped pacing, leaned against the trunk of an ancient palm tree. Who was he kidding? From the moment he had stepped aboard Abdullah's plane and been confronted by a pair of frankly assessing brown eyes he had been hooked.

She had something special. The something special that made people turn on the evening news for her report from the latest trouble spot. The something special that made people care about her. And, close up, he'd discovered what it was.

She had a vulnerability beneath the toughness. Laughed more readily than she wept.

Even when she wanted to weep more than anything else.

She'd come close to spilling out her grief today. He'd wanted to hold her, comfort her. He wanted to know what kind of man would bring that look to her eyes... Wanted to be that man.

'Yes...hello...' A groggy voice broke into his thoughts.

'Partridge?' he said sharply.

'Excellency?' There was a fumbling sound, a crash. 'What's happened? What's wrong?'

'Nothing is happening,' he said. 'That's what's wrong.' His irritation iced the distance between them. 'Have you found him yet?'

'Excellency, I'll let you know when I find him. But it's four o'clock in the morning here...'

'So?' he snapped.

'So I didn't get to bed until two,' Partridge snapped right back, fully awake now, his hackles rising fast. 'The best information I have is that Faisal is holed up in some cabin in the Adirondacks with a girl. But no one is saying which girl, or what cabin, and there are a heck of a lot of them. Since they're not all arranged in a neat little row along a paved road, it's taking time to check them out.' He paused. 'And while we're discussing missing persons, how *is* Miss Fenton?' Hassan smiled, if a little grimly, at his aide's edgy sarcasm. If he'd heard about Rose's abduction it went a long way to explaining Partridge's unusually quick temper. 'I assume her disappearance is down to you? It's all over CNN that she's missing.'

Well, that was something. 'And who are they suggesting is responsible?'

'No one seems to have a clue. Or if they do they're not saying. Abdullah's line seems to be that she must have wandered away from Tim's car while he was hunting for the horse and got lost, or that maybe she's fallen into a gully.'

'Rose Fenton? They can't be serious.'

'It's a lot more palatable than admitting that she might have been kidnapped. You said you wouldn't do anything…like that.'

Like what? Just what did Partridge think he was doing to his heroine of the airwaves?

'Did I? I remember the conversation somewhat differently. However, you can rest assured that Miss Fenton is in good health and perfectly happy to remain as my guest.' There was a distinctly un-aide-like noise down the line. 'Your concern is misplaced, believe me. She's more than capable of dealing with the situation. In fact I'd say she's taking full advantage of being in the centre of a breaking story and playing the situation to her own advantage. And I promise you she's in no danger.'

'No?' Partridge was clearly not convinced, but then they both knew he wasn't concerned about physical danger. His reputation might be exaggerated but Hassan was the first to admit that there had been a lot to exaggerate.

'Did you know that she's been married?' he asked, cruelly needing to puncture Partridge's precious image of the woman. Hassan knew he'd assume that she was divorced. The lack of a response suggested that he'd hit a nerve. Then, angry with himself, he said, 'Why don't you call your contacts in London and find out what you can about him?' That he had died, that she grieved, that her place on the pedestal was safe. 'With all the interest in her right now, it shouldn't be difficult.'

'Is that an order or a suggestion?' Only Partridge could bristle long distance.

'I don't make suggestions,' he replied curtly. 'And in the meantime, if you're so worried about Rose Fenton's welfare, I suggest you find Faisal and get him back here without delay. Then you have my permission to come back and tell me to my face exactly what you're thinking right now.'

'I don't need your permission for that,' he said stiffly. 'And when I've told you, you'll have my resignation.'

'You can challenge me a to a duel if it will make you happy, but not until you've found Faisal.'

Rose crossed to the tent and went inside, glad to be out of the sun. She unwound the *keffiyeh*, tossed aside the cloak and pushed her fingers through her hair, lifting it from her neck.

She was hot and dusty, the cloth of her shirt sticking to her back. What she needed was a shower, followed by a dip in the deep, cool water of the sports club pool. The shower was empty and the pool was hours away. All that left was the stream, and she had the feeling that the stream would be off limits unless Hassan gave the word. And Hassan wasn't there to ask.

When they'd arrived back at the encampment, he'd paused only long enough to see her safely dismounted and under cover before wheeling his horse and riding away. Visiting his communications centre, no doubt, to find out how his plans were progressing, she'd thought crossly, and she'd watched him disappear behind the thick fringe of palm trees, a couple of his men falling in behind him.

He could have taken her with him. It hurt that he hadn't; she'd thought he'd begun to accept her as a partner in his plot. More fool her.

Well, she had her own communications centre, and she'd jolly well use it, too. She poured some water into a bowl and washed her hands and face. Then she poured herself a glass of iced tea from a vacuum flask. She'd call her mother first. And she'd check her voice mail.

Gordon would undoubtedly have left a message for her. Several messages, possibly. No one else would have thought of that. No one else knew she had the phone.

She stood for a while beneath the wide awning, sipping her tea, looking out across the oasis. It was so peaceful here. In the quiet heat even the dogs had the wisdom not to waste energy in useless barking.

Don't stand when you can sit; don't sit when you can

lie. In the drugging stillness of midday the philosophy held a certain appeal, and she was tempted into a canvas safari chair left in the shade of the awning.

Hassan's Saluki stretched himself at her feet, while below her the endless desert gave the impression that there was all the time in the world. It was actually rather difficult to get herself worked up about anything beyond the empty horizon. She just wanted to stay here, ride, talk.

Make love.

'*A Flask of Wine, a Book of Verse—and Thou Beside me singing in the Wilderness—*' Down there beside the stream, she thought. Beneath the palm trees and the pomegranates, where they would be hidden from the world by the thicket of oleanders. He'd have a silk carpet spread for her and soft cushions. Because the 'Thou' was unquestionably Hassan.

Dangerous. Trouble. But he made her blood sing.

Make love.

The words had popped into her head unbidden but now refused to budge.

Make love.

It was a long time since love had appeared on her life's want list. Nearly six long years since she'd found Michael where he'd fallen and died in the paddock. It had been quick, the doctor had told her later. His heart had been a time bomb waiting to go off and even if she'd been with him she could have done nothing to save him.

His children had blamed her for what had happened, though. Not as much as she'd blamed herself. But the doctor had been right. Michael had known the risk and he'd taken it without burdening her, given her what she'd needed. He'd been so gentle. So kind. And she'd made him happy. She had nothing to reproach herself for.

And now Hassan had reminded her that life went on. That she was a young woman with hot blood pumping through her veins. The next time he decided to play the savage, she vowed, he wouldn't get off so lightly. And as she set down her glass she realised that she was smiling.

Hassan cut the connection, tossed the phone to the man holding his horse, mounted and rode hard back towards the oasis, hoping that physical effort would dull the need, cool the seething cauldron of emotions brought to the boil by Rose Fenton.

He'd met women who could turn a man's head at fifty paces. Women who could heat a man's blood with a look. But he'd never met anyone like Rose.

Those other women had looked at him, smiled at him, flirted with him, but they'd never seen beyond the jeweller's case in his pocket. And it hadn't mattered. Yet he couldn't even bear to hear Rose Fenton's name on his aide's lips, knowing that Partridge honoured her with his esteem, while he wanted to keep her hidden away, keep her just for himself like some old-style sultan.

She was right. It was a primitive way to behave. But it was the only way he knew, while Rose Fenton was a modern woman, the daughter of a prominent feminist, a woman in control of her own life, moulded for the twenty-first century.

They came from very different worlds and he was forced to confront the vastness of the gulf that lay between them. It was nothing that wealth or power could surmount. It was fundamental, part of who they were.

It made him angry. Restless. He wanted her so much that his skin felt two sizes too small for his body; worse was his certainty that she knew it. From the look in her eyes it wouldn't take much to tempt her to share the bed with him. But it would be on her terms and not his. In a week or two she would go away, resume her career, get on with her life. She would have marked him for ever, while she would go about her business and he would quickly be forgotten, blurred with a dozen other casual encounters.

He realised that his hands were clenched into fists, the knuckle bones white against his skin, and he took a slow, deep breath, stretched his fingers, forcing himself to let go of the thought. Thinking about it was not a good idea. He refused to think about it. He would stay away from her. He had enough problems demanding his total concentration.

More easily said than done. All he'd wanted was to keep her out of Abdullah's way, create sufficient mayhem while he got Faisal home and produced him for his people with the world's press looking on.

Instead she'd taken possession of every one of his senses, robbed him of the ability to concentrate on his purpose.

He'd touched her and couldn't wash away the scent of her skin. The husky whisper of her voice was a constant echo in his head. He knew, deep down, that for the rest of his life all he would have to do was close his eyes and she would be there. One moment indignant, the next laughing at him and with him, then looking at him with eyes that eclipsed the sun so that he wanted to stop all the pretence and make her his willing prisoner, bind her to his side and keep her there for ever.

He'd been brought up to accept that an arranged marriage, where both parties acknowledged a parity of purpose, had more chance of fulfilment than some chance encounter with a stranger. He had accepted it; he knew it could work. Nadeem was happy. Leila, his younger sister, was content. He knew it and yet had still resisted every attempt by his family to persuade him that this girl, or that, would be the perfect wife for him.

And yet he'd never believed in sentimental love. Never believed in that instant of recognition when a man saw the one woman who had it in her power to make him happy for the rest of his life.

Until now, when the emptiness of a future without Rose Fenton at his side appalled him.

It was crazy. Ridiculous. Impossible.

He opened his eyes and let the precious image go. As he would have to let her go. She belonged to the world, while he belonged here. Maybe Nadeem was right. It was time to take a wife, raise sons, stake his place in the future of his country. Faisal would need someone he could trust at his back.

And in the meantime he'd keep his distance from the lovely Rose Fenton. He'd supposedly come to the desert to hunt. Maybe it was time he took the hawks and the dogs into the desert. Time to put some distance between himself and the woman he might have but could never keep.

It was an appealing idea. Unfortunately life was not that simple. He had brought her here, and, although he knew she would protest the fact, he simply could not leave her without his protection.

Ahead of him lay his encampment, spread around the oasis. His own huge tent set a little way apart. He steered clear of it, walking his horse to the edge of the water with the intention of plunging in to cool his overheated skin, his overheated brain.

A shout distracted him, and as he turned he saw one of his men hurrying towards him.

Rose sighed, glanced at her watch and realised she'd been sitting there longer than she'd realised.

Wool gathering. Her mind had been wandering, wasting precious time. What on earth was the matter with her? She'd quickly stiffened up and groaned as she straightened. She'd forgotten how hard riding was on the muscles after a long break.

The horse liniment seemed more and more appealing. Or maybe it was just the thought of Hassan applying it. She shouldn't have been so quick to turn him down, she thought, wincing as she reached for the tissue box. Then she frowned.

She'd left everything in a muddle last night, but it had been tidied, dusted, polished. Everything put back neatly. She glanced around. Someone had been in there. Someone had folded away her nightdress, taken away the *shalwar kameez*, straightened the bed.

In a sudden panic she grabbed for the box, but even as she thrust her hand inside she knew it was pointless.

'Is this what you're looking for?'

She spun around. Hassan let the curtain fall behind him, advanced on her, the little cellphone gripped between the thumb and forefinger of his hand.

For a moment she couldn't think of a thing to say; he knew the answer and there didn't seem much point in stating the obvious. But since he was clearly expecting some kind of response she lifted her shoulders in the slightest of shrugs and said, 'Oh, bother.' Then, because that didn't appear to satisfy him, 'I hadn't anticipated you'd have a resident Mrs Mopp.'

CHAPTER SEVEN

HASSAN didn't respond with one of those wry smiles he did so well when he was really making an effort. Maybe he wasn't in the mood for flippant humour. And who could blame him?

'Who have you called, Rose?' he asked quietly, with admirable self-control. 'More importantly, what have you told them?'

Well, that was easy, although whether he would believe her was another matter entirely. 'No one,' she said, deciding that this would be a good time to keep strictly to the point. 'And nothing.'

'You expect me to believe that?'

It would be nice, just once in a while, to be surprised, she thought. Not that she blamed him for doubting her probity. She'd have doubted her probity if she'd been in his shoes. It made her all the more determined to stick to the truth.

'It wasn't for want of trying,' she assured him. 'I couldn't get through to my mother last night. Not surprisingly, the line was engaged. It probably still is. And I didn't want to put my brother in a situation where he would have to try and hide the truth. He'd do his best if I asked him to, but the poor lamb couldn't fool a baby.'

'Why would he have to hide the truth?'

'Well, I couldn't tell him where I was, only who'd abducted me, and that didn't seem like a good idea.'

That earned her an odd look, but he let it go. 'But your news desk? Surely you called them?'

She pulled a face. 'I should have done. Gordon will be livid. But all I could tell them was that you'd abducted me—'

'You're saying you wouldn't?' he demanded. 'Wouldn't tell your news editor? Couldn't tell your brother? Why?'

Looking at it from his perspective, she could see his problem. 'I thought I'd find out why you did it first. Before I brought Abdullah's storm troopers crashing around your ears.'

'Oh, right.' He finally succumbed to deep sarcasm.

Well, Rose didn't blame him for that, either, but it occurred to her that she might be able to prove it. She held out her hand. 'Give me the phone.'

'You're kidding?'

'That's my line. Give me the phone and I'll prove I haven't made any calls.' He didn't seem to think that was a particularly good idea. 'If I've already called for the cavalry, Hassan, it's too late to do anything about it now. Give me the phone.'

He surrendered it with a shrug and she quickly punched in the code for her voice mail. There were three messages from Gordon. The last one, giving a special number that would be manned twenty-four hours a day, was timed at less than an hour earlier. While she'd been sitting sipping iced tea and wool gathering and her phone had been long gone. She held it out for Hassan to listen as the messages were repeated.

'Pretty conclusive, wouldn't you say?'

Hassan didn't answer, simply snapped the cellphone shut, pocketed it, and stared at her as if trying to decide what she was up to. Well, she didn't think he was the kind of man who spent too much time grovelling for forgiveness. It probably wouldn't even occur to him.

'Okay,' she said, 'I'll forgo the apology, but I want my network to have an exclusive on the whole story. That's only fair. And you're going to need some help to get the media coverage you want at just the right moment. I could organise that...'

It was eminently reasonable and, considering what he'd put her through, he should have been on his knees thanking her. Instead he looked like something straight out of a thundercloud. Dark and menacing and given to sudden, intemperate outbursts.

'You know what you are, don't you?' he said flatly, ignoring her offer. She thought she did, but decided that since nothing was going to stop him from telling her she might as well save her breath. 'You're an idiot.'

Close, she thought. There was room for 'complete and utter' in there somewhere, but brevity was good. It was one of the hallmarks of a good journalist.

'I can't believe that you'd be so stupid.' Ah. He hadn't finished. Like all amateurs, he didn't recognise the perfect place to stop. 'So irresponsible. So...so...'

'Dumb?' she offered.

Bad move. He practically exploded. 'You had the means to get yourself out of here but decided, in the best tradition of some girls' own comic book heroine, that you just had to go for the story. Is that it?'

'Hassan—'

'Rose Fenton, Ace Reporter.'

'Oh, puh-leeze!'

'Never misses a deadline. Never misses a scoop.'
Actually, Rose thought, that was rather good, but before
she could tell him so he continued. 'You don't know
me,' he swept on, brushing aside her attempt to interrupt him. 'You could have had no idea what I planned
to do with you.'

She opened her mouth to tell him that he didn't look
like a white slave trader, but his eyebrows warned her
that it had better be good. And, hey, who knew what a
white slave trader looked like?

She could, of course, tell him that she'd done her
homework on him and she'd been deeply attracted to
the idea of writing a feature article on the disinherited
prince. She could explain that his abduction had happily
short-circuited her unsuccessful efforts to meet him. Or
even that seeing him as he boarded the plane to Ras al
Hajar, the moment when they had exchanged that brief
look, had jarred something loose in her brain so that
she had finally remembered she wasn't just a journalist,
she was a woman.

Perhaps not.

'What the hell were you thinking, Rose?' *Thinking?*
Oh, well, that was different. It didn't take much to work
out that she hadn't been doing any serious thinking
since she boarded that plane... 'What happens the next
time someone grabs you in the dark? Will you glibly
tell yourself that there's nothing to worry about because
everything was fine last time? Will you think, What the
heck? Hassan was a real gentleman and I got a pay rise
on the back of the story?' She waited. Silence. 'Well?'

She flinched from the sudden whip-crack of his voice. He'd finally got it all off his chest and now he was impatient for an explanation of her aberrant behaviour.

Unfortunately it was impossible to explain why she'd followed her instincts instead of discretion without revealing more of herself than she cared to, at least not while he was angry with her.

'Actually, you know, I'm not so sure about the gentleman bit,' Rose said. 'Last night you were...' No, forget last night. 'And as for the pay rise.' She shrugged. 'Who knows? I didn't call the news desk when I could have, should have, and you haven't promised me that exclusive yet. If I don't get it you can forget the pay rise; I'll probably be looking for another job.'

A hiss of something like outrage escaped his teeth, and as Hassan grabbed her arms and hauled her up, so that her face was within an inch of his, Rose decided that she'd finally pushed her luck to the limit.

Maybe just a bit beyond.

'All right, all right,' she said quickly. 'I *am* stupid. Very stupid. Famous for it. Ask anyone.' Then, slowly and carefully, 'If you'll just put me down and return my phone, I'll call for a taxi and leave you in peace.'

For a moment he continued to hold her, her toes barely touching the ground as he held her up against him, head to head, face to face, warning her, challenging her. And in the shadowy light of the softly filtered sunlight the mood subtly altered.

His swift flare of anger died back to a dull glow. She felt the heat of it lick over her, bypassing her clothes and going straight for the skin. She felt breathless, weak, and her mouth softened, parted, wanting more than anything for him to kiss her. To hold her. To love her.

If he cared that much, it shouldn't be impossible. If she could just touch him, touch his face, reach for his hand, she could make him see that.

But her arms were clamped to her sides, and after a moment Hassan very carefully lowered her to the ground, steadied her while she found her balance and then took his hands from her arms. Only then did he take a step back.

'Taxis...' His voice was shaking, she realised. Well, that was okay. She was shaking everywhere, and if he was going for control this time she wanted to be sure that he was having a really tough time resisting the primeval pull of a need that had them both in its grip.

She was wrong about him not being a gentleman. He was being too much of a gentleman. He'd slipped once but he wouldn't again. Not without unbearable provocation. Perhaps seeing the intent in her eyes, he took a further step back.

'Taxis?' she prompted, stepping after him, hoping to goad him into ignoring the consequences, to see heat turn his granite eyes to molten lava.

'This isn't Chelsea, Rose. There are no taxis here.' Almost, she thought. Almost. But it would take more than words to drive him over the edge and he wouldn't let her touch him. He wouldn't risk coming that close again.

'Oh, well,' she said. 'Just a thought.' And when he'd backed out of the sleeping quarters and the air was no longer humming with unspoken threats, unspoken desires. She added, 'I guess that means I'll be stopping.'

Then she sat down rather abruptly on the bed. She'd lost her phone but she didn't care. This wasn't about the story any more. All right. So, it was a great story. Any other time she would be chasing it down like a speeding bullet. But if she was patient, and stayed where she was, the story would come to her.

And besides, she was supposed to be on holiday.

What had he said as he made her his captive? A little pleasure, a little romance? Well, right now a little romance was exactly what she wanted.

It was a just a pity that for once in his life the playboy prince had decided to behave himself. In theory, she applauded his decision to reform. In practice, she wasn't too happy about the timing, even if she understood the reason for it.

He'd carried her off without so much as a by-your-leave-ma'am and now he felt responsible for her. So be it.

She lay back against the pillows and smiled. He was responsible for her and it was up to her to make sure that he took his reponsibilities very seriously.

'You can't just kiss and run, Hassan,' she murmured softly into the quiet of the midday heat. 'I won't let you.'

Given a second chance, Hassan wasted no time in cooling himself off. He scooped a pail full of water from the trough pumped up for the horses and poured it over his head.

Such an action would normally have provoked ribald

mockery from men he had grown up with, known all his life. It spoke volumes that not one of them so much as grinned at his discomfort. Not that he had much inclination to congratulate himself.

Rose Fenton provoked agitation simply by breathing. Refused to sit quietly in the shadows and wait. She'd have her story. She knew that. But she was going to make him pay for his impertinence.

He wished he'd never heard of her. Wished she'd never come to Ras al Hajar. Wished, wished, wished...

His men were waiting for his orders. He gave them, and wished he could dispense with his own problems as easily.

Then he realised that he could. Or dispense with one of them. He could call Nadeem, accept her offer to keep Rose safe for a few days, and she could flutter those long lashes from now until kingdom come but he wouldn't change his mind. He took the small cellphone from his pocket and switched it on. He'd do it now.

His sister finally came to the phone, not happy at being called from the clinic she ran in the poorest quarter of the city. 'What is it, Hassan? I'm busy.'

'I know, and I'm sorry, but I want you to...need you to...' Damn it, no, he didn't. Couldn't.

'What's the matter, my brother? Is your lady journalist getting a little too hot for you to handle?' Her soft, knowing laughter held a touch of sympathy that caught him momentarily off balance.

But, while Rose Fenton was searing him down to the bone, he wasn't about to admit it to his little sister. 'No. It's simply that on reflection I think you are right.'

'Well, there has to be a first time for everything. Right about what?'

He hesitated for no more than a heartbeat. 'About marriage. I believe it's time I had a wife.'

'Hassan!' She made no effort to disguise her astonishment or her delight at the news.

'I shall have to stay here once Faisal is back. He'll need someone he can rely on.'

'And you will need someone to keep you warm in that big cold fort you call a home.'

The idea filled him with a chill far deeper than the stone walls of the fort could ever achieve. 'Arrange it, will you?'

'Do you have anyone particular in mind? Or perhaps Miss Fenton wishes to press her claim?'

'Please be serious, Nadeem.'

'I was being perfectly serious. She has a claim on you. I cannot speak to anyone else until that is settled.'

'I'll settle it, Nadeem, but in the meantime will you look for some quiet girl who doesn't answer back?' Nadeem was silent for so long that he was afraid that he had betrayed himself. 'A girl who will be a suitable mother for my sons,' he said abruptly. 'I'm sure you know where to lay your hands upon a list of suitable virgins.'

'Leave it with me, Hassan,' she said, rather more gently. 'I'll see if I can find someone you will like.'

'You've nagged me for long enough. Don't make me wait now.' He snapped the phone shut. A man must marry eventually, and if he couldn't have the woman he wanted then he would learn to want the woman he had. But he didn't want too long to dwell on the difference.

Then, with a sigh, he opened the phone again. He called up the memory and punched in Pam Fenton's number.

Rose washed away the dust from her wild ride, searched the trunk for something loose and cool to wear in the heat of the afternoon and all the time, beyond the drapes, she heard soft movements in the living quarters as the table was prepared for lunch. But Hassan did not return. She had not expected him to.

After a while there was a quiet cough from beyond the curtain. 'You wish to eat, *sitti*?'

Sitti? My lady?

Startled by such courtesy, such honour, Rose quickly got up, draped a long silk chiffon scarf modestly about her head and emerged. The table, as she'd suspected, was laid for one. There was meat. Unleavened bread, freshly baked. A tabbouleh. Thick slices of tomato.

'*Sukran,*' she said, making use of one of the few words of Arabic she had learned. 'Thank you. It looks delicious.' The man bowed. 'But I'd like to eat down there. By the stream.' She didn't wait for his protest, but walked past him as if there was no question but that he would follow her.

'*Sitti…*' He chased after her as she swept out of the tent. She pretended not to hear, concentrating on keeping safe on the rocky path. '*Sitti,*' he implored. 'The food is here.' She kept going. 'Tomorrow,' he offered. 'Tomorrow, *insh'Allah*, I will take the food to the stream for you.'

She stopped, turned to look up at him and his face relaxed. Then she looked back to the stream.

'Just there,' she said, indicating the spot she had chosen for her picnic. And walked on.

Behind her there was a buzz of consternation, and Rose smiled with satisfaction. They could not stop her. She was *sitti*, my lady, their lady, and, by a process of elimination, Hassan's lady. They could not leave her to wander off by herself. She might hurt herself. She might try to run away.

But neither could they restrain her. Only Hassan could do that.

It wasn't her problem; it was theirs. She was sure they'd work something out.

Meantime, she sat on a large flat rock above one of the streams that fed the oasis, pulled off the sandals she had been wearing when she had been carried off and dangled her feet in the water.

It was blissfully cool. She leaned back on her hands, lifted her face to the light breeze blowing from the mountains. Later, she thought, she would bathe.

A man armed with a rifle appeared and stationed himself a little distance away, taking care never to quite look in her direction. She wondered what the gun was for. Were there snakes? Or was he hoping for some small gazelle to wander down to the water and provide him with an easy meal.

After a while two men appeared on the edge of her vision, walking towards a shady spot at the stream's edge. They were bearing a large carpet which they spread over the ground. They kept their eyes averted.

She pretended not to notice, sure that any attention from her would embarrass them.

Cushions were brought.

She swished her feet in the water. It had felt strange, putting on a floor-length gown in the middle of the day, but sitting beside the stream, the featherweight silk of her caftan clinging to her legs, trailing in the water, she felt rather like a fairytale princess.

The food arrived, packed in two carrying boxes. Her heart picked up a beat. Would he come? Or had he left the camp, ridden away into the desert where she couldn't torment him.

Or was she fooling herself? Maybe he'd heard from Faisal...

The sun was shimmering on the slate-blue silk of her dress, lighting her hair through the gauzy film of her scarf. Hassan fought to catch his breath as he watched her from a distance, tried to feel nothing.

Impossible.

Trailing her toes in the water, she looked too much like some exotic princess from the *Arabian Nights*. Scheherazade could not have been more beautiful as she spun her web of stories. They had that in common. And cleverness.

His male-dominated society would jar against the bedrock of her feminist upbringing, but she would happily use its conventions to her advantage.

Life would never be dull with her around to torment him. And there would be endless days like this, with Rose waiting for him.

He let the dream fade. Not endless days. How long

before she was fretting for more, for the life she knew, the freedom?

They would have a few weeks of joy, but he would not be able to keep her. And he would not be able to let her go. They would both be trapped.

A shadow fell across her and Rose looked up. Hassan had dismissed the guard and was holding the rifle, waiting, his expression so distant that they might have been in different worlds. She looked away without acknowledging his presence.

'Is that what you wanted?' he asked finally.

Not quite. But it was a start. She offered him her hand. He had no choice but to take it, wrapping strong fingers around her palm to help her to her feet. But the moment she was standing, he released it.

Different galaxies.

'You're wet,' she said.

'I was hot.'

'Hot.' She repeated the word as if unsure of the meaning.

'And dusty. You had possession of my bathroom so I used a bucket.'

'Fully clothed? I thought that kind of modesty was reserved for your women?' Oh, damn. That was no way to woo a prince. She really would have to concentrate. She picked up her sandals and, with her wet hem trailing in the dust, led the way down to the waiting picnic, where she settled herself somewhat self-consciously among the cushions, tucking her feet out of sight and feeling uncomfortably theatrical, like some mythical *houri*.

But so far, so good. She'd got the picnic and she'd got Hassan. Except that he'd taken himself to a nearby rock, where he was sitting, looking away to the distant mountains, merely waiting for her to eat her lunch and grow bored with the game she was playing.

She opened one of the picnic boxes. 'What's the gun for?' she asked, as she examined the contents.

'Leopards. Panthers.'

She'd heard there were cats in the mountains, but thought it unlikely they would come so close to people. 'You kill them?'

'If they attack the animals.' She glanced up. 'They do, occasionally,' he said, apparently sensing her doubt. 'And if the choice was between you and one of them, then, yes, I would shoot to kill. Despite the temptation to leave you to your fate.' She tutted. 'A warning shot would probably be enough,' he conceded.

'I was commenting on your hospitality, not your wildlife management policies.'

'Is something wrong with the food?' he asked, being deliberately obtuse.

'No. It's delicious, but far too much for one.'

'It's probably my cook's way of suggesting you are too thin.'

'I didn't think he was supposed to notice.'

'You have a way of attracting attention.'

Maybe, but not his, she thought, as he kept his gaze fixed on the middle distance. And twenty feet between them. She rolled onto her back and watched the perfect blue of the sky through the branches of the pomegranates.

'Have you heard from Faisal?' she asked.

'Not yet.'

'Maybe he's already on his way?'

'I wish that were so, but Partridge is still looking for him.'

'And when he finds him? Then what? Will you have a press conference? Now you've got the undivided attention of the press?'

'I thought maybe you would like to introduce the new Emir to the world?'

'It would make a great story.'

'Short of World War III breaking out, I'd imagine that the missing journalist appearing with the youthful Emir in tow would pretty much guarantee the front page.'

'Probably.' But she was tired of the story. She wanted Hassan. 'There's a bird up there,' she said, after a moment. 'I've never seen anything like it. What is it?'

'Describe it.'

He was playing hard to get, but she wasn't going anywhere. 'Did you ever read *The Bluebird of Happiness* when you were a child?' she asked quietly, so as not to disturb the bird. If she'd hoped to draw him nearer, she was disappointed.

'It's a European folk-tale,' he replied dismissively.

He was determined to keep some distance between them, even if it was only cultural. She continued to gaze up into the branches of the tree. 'I thought your Scottish grandmother might have read it to you. You did visit Scotland?'

There was the slightest pause. 'Often. But you already knew that, didn't you?'

And he knew about the bluebird, or he would not have dismissed it in quite that way. But she didn't challenge him on it.

'The bluebird is an allegory for something wonderful that you search for all your life, only to discover that it's right there, under your nose, all the time.' He made no comment. 'It's like that,' she murmured.

'What is?'

He was distracted, which was promising. 'The bird. It's bright blue.' As she spoke, the bird swooped away in a low, looping flight.

'It's a roller. A lilac-breasted roller,' he said, watching the bird's flight from the safe distance of his rock. 'Eat your lunch, Rose.'

She closed her eyes. Bother. Double bother. 'It's too hot to eat. I think I'll bathe.'

'Bathe?' Was it her imagination or did she detect a note of concern in his voice?

'You listed bathing in the stream as one of the attractions. Riding, bathing, lying in the sun.' She ticked them off on her fingers. 'Well, I've ridden, I've lain in the sun, and now I want to swim. Afterwards I'll eat. If you're not hungry, you can sing to me.'

'Not a good idea. I've remembered, it's definitely a crow.'

'I'll be the judge of that. Beauty, after all, is in the ear of the listener.'

She stood up, and the simple, flowing caftan shimmered about her, falling loosely from her shoulders. The neckline was modestly scooped and it was fastened with tiny silk buttons from neck to hem, dozens of them. She began to unfasten them, starting at the top and taking her time. One. Two.

'What on earth do you think you're doing?' he demanded. He was on his feet now and a step closer. He could come close enough to stop her, or her could stand there and watch her strip down to some very sexy underwear and swim. This was wild country, and someone had to keep an eye on her. He'd already made that point.

She slipped another button. Three. 'I'm going to dunk myself in that stream.' She almost felt sorry for him. Four.

'There may be snakes in the water.'

Sneaky. 'What are the odds that one will bite me?' she asked. He didn't answer. More buttons. Five. Six. The dress was beginning to part over her bosom, the sun to bite at her skin. She hadn't thought to put sunblock down so far, but it was too late to worry about that now. 'And if one does bite me, will I die?'

'It would be painful.'

She wasn't practised in seductive disrobing but his face assured her that she was doing just fine. He wanted to look away. He really wanted to. But he couldn't do that, any more than he could lie to her. Not even to save himself from this. Her fingers trembled on the next button. It twisted and she had to look down, untangle it.

He was closer. Without looking, she knew he was closer. The down on her skin prickled with the closeness of him; sweat started on her lip.

She licked it away, struggled with the twisted cord.

His fingers fastened about her wrist, stopping her. 'What do you want, Rose?'

She wanted him. Body, heart and soul.

She wanted to lift her hand to his face, lay her palm against his cheek, rest her head against his chest and hear the slow reassurance of his heartbeat. She wanted him so much that the heat of it licked against her thighs, and she longed to lie on the cushions with him beside her, shaded by the trees for all the long afternoon while they learned all there was to know about each other.

The moment was perfect for it, but he seemed set on refusing to accept the gift of it, of her. The distance he was trying to keep between them, however, suggested he wasn't finding the sacrifice of desire to honourable necessity that easy. Well, she hadn't meant him to.

Ashamed of herself, and with an effort of will that sent a shudder running through her, she smiled. 'I simply wanted your attention, Hassan.'

'You have it,' he assured her. 'Fasten those buttons and you'll keep it.' Rose was tempted to suggest that leaving them the way they were was doing the job just fine. That was the trouble with Hassan. He was infinitely tempting. But she would be good, even if his hand about her wrist was making it impossible to do as he asked. She gestured helplessly with her free hand, but he hadn't finished. 'And when you've done that, maybe you'll tell me what you really want, Rose.'

CHAPTER EIGHT

HASSAN kept asking all the right questions, Rose thought a little desperately, but somehow the answers weren't connecting.

'An interview,' she said, desperately improvising. Since she was clearly hopeless at seduction, maybe it was time to try what she did best. 'You're going to be news in a day or two, and since I'm stuck here at your convenience, and you're stuck with me until Faisal arrives, we might as well take advantage of the situation.'

'We? You seem to be doing just fine all on your own.' His gaze, until then kept firmly upon her face, drifted slowly down, stopping only when confronted with the gaping front of the caftan. What the sun had been doing to her skin was nothing compared to the scorching heat of his eyes. He switched his gaze so quickly that she almost gasped aloud as he looked up, confronting her head on. 'Or maybe you always strip off for interviews?'

Tempted to toss off the smart-alecky response—*it depends who I'm interviewing*—Rose restrained herself. She didn't want Hassan getting the idea she made a habit of it. On the other hand, the *whatever it takes* response sounded positively reckless.

And this wasn't reckless? This dry-mouthed, heart-pounding, hanging-herself-out-to-dry seduction routine wasn't reckless? Well, she had a name to live up to.

'Front-line' Fenton always gets her interview. She had yet to claim the man.

'I had to get your attention somehow,' she managed finally.

A muscle worked in the corner of his mouth. 'Believe me, you've got it.' Or it might just have been the beginnings of a smile... It was there for a second and gone before she could be quite certain. But every journey begins with a single step, and she did have his attention. Now she must make the best use of it she knew how.

'Then let's get down to work.'

'It's all been done before,' he warned her, and there was no almost-smile to show that he didn't care. He cared.

'Not the way I'm going to write it.' She wasn't out to destroy him. 'I'm going to write about you, Hassan al Rashid, so that when Faisal is Emir you can be at his right hand and people will not remember you as a rebel without a cause, kicking over the traces because you didn't get your heart's desire, but as a steadfast brother and friend.'

'You're planning to redeem my shattered reputation single-handed?' She could feel the tension drain from him, the fast hold he had on her wrist loosen as his brow creased in confusion. 'What with?'

'Time, patience. Your co-operation.' Reckless was back, but she couldn't help herself. He did that to her. 'You *will* co-operate?'

'I don't appear to have a choice.' There was a long, dizzying pause when he seemed to hang on the edge of some precipice.

Diamonds. Yellow diamonds to match her tiger eyes. Hassan wanted to strip her naked and then dress her in nothing but precious gems, bind her to him with ropes of pearls, make sweet love to her on a bed of rose petals. For a moment he thought he would faint from his desperate need for this woman. It was as if he had been waiting for her all his life. Was it always to be like this? He could have anything in the world but his heart's desire…

'Hassan?'

The hesitant, slightly anxious note in her voice pulled him back from the brink of madness. It was time to finish it, put a stop to foolish dreams.

'I'm sorry, I was just wondering… Would it help, do you think, if you had pictures of my wedding to go with your article?'

'Your wedding?' She began to laugh. Hassan didn't join in, and he knew the exact moment when Rose recognised that he had not been speaking hypothetically. Her entire body stilled, her skin flushed, the huge black pupils of her eyes seemed rimmed with topaz-gold in the clear, bright air. How could he resist her? The words clamoured in his head. *I love you. I want you with me, always.* It was the 'always' that was the problem. Maybe she saw that in his face, because she seemed almost to shrink away from him. 'Wedding?' She repeated the word uncertainly.

'Nadeem is right,' he said, with a casual lack of interest that he knew would disgust her, that he did not have to fake. 'I will have to stay here now, with Faisal, and a man must have sons. I've asked her to find me a suitable bride. Someone quiet,' he said, and heard the words as if they were spoken at a great distance, by someone else. 'Someone who doesn't answer back.'

There was a long, still moment during which Rose withdrew her wrist from his grasp and pulled her dress tightly about her, fumbling at the buttons, giving up and clutching the edges together. The sunlight shimmered on her skin like gold dust, her hair was like fire, but she looked cold, and as he looked on, helpless to do anything, she shivered.

'Sons?' She repeated the word with contempt. He longed to take her into his arms and hold her, to tell her how much he desired her, wanted her. It took everything that was good in him to hold back. 'And what happens if you just get daughters?' she asked, her boldness undermined by the faintest quiver to her voice. 'Will you trade her in for another model?'

'No, I won't do that. There would be no point, since the sex of the offspring is determined by the man.' What would be the point when one woman who was not Rose would be the same as any other woman?

'I know that. I wasn't sure that you did. Don't most primitive men blame their women for a lack of male children? But then, what sperm would dare defy your wishes?'

Her mockery was savage. If only he could tell her what he'd give to have daughters like her. Each named for a flower like their mother. But he wasn't in the business of making her think of him as late-twentieth-century man. He wasn't. Not in any way that mattered.

'That is in the hands of Allah, Rose.'

'Oh, I see.' Her irony was barbed. 'Well, then, I can see why it doesn't matter who you marry.'

Beneath the careless posture, he flinched at her scorn. Then tossed more fuel on the fire. 'Who says it doesn't matter? Family ties. Land. Dowry. These things matter a great deal.'

'That's positively medieval.'

'If you believe that, you'll find a soulmate in Simon Partridge,' he said, and felt murderously primitive at the thought of her finding a soulmate in any man but himself. 'He assures me that I'm galloping at full speed into the fourteenth century.'

'Then why does he work for you?'

'He doesn't. At least he won't once he's brought Faisal home. He took grave exception to the way I abducted you.'

'Then you're right, Hassan. We'll get along just fine.'

He wanted to take her hand. Hold it between his and tell her that this wasn't the way he wanted it. Try to make her see that this was the way it had to be. And he finally understood how helpless his grandfather must have felt all those years ago, bitterly ashamed that he hadn't been mature enough to accept his decision and make an old man's last few weeks on earth peaceful.

Instead, he gestured for her to sit.

For a moment she defied him, then crumpled onto the cushions as if her legs had suddenly given way. She'd forgotten about the buttons. Her dress gaped slightly to offer a hint of lace, to torment him with the soft swell of her breast.

Maybe he deserved it, but in need of distraction he took some bread, filled it with lamb and tabbouleh and salad and offered it to her. She took it, he suspected, simply because it was too much effort to argue. She took it and held it almost defensively, but made no attempt to eat.

He filled another piece of bread for himself, not because he was hungry, but because without something to occupy his hands he was afraid they would finish what Rose had started.

It wasn't much to constrain a man. A piece of bread and an unknown bride without name or substance to stand between him and everything he desired.

'Tell me about your family.' She'd put down the bread. Maybe she wasn't hungry. Maybe it was too much effort to hold it. Maybe all her strength was being channelled into an effort to keep her voice steady. If he hadn't been able to see her, the voice would have fooled him. 'Did your mother love your father?'

'Rose—'

'I know she didn't choose who she would marry, but did she love him?' She looked up sharply, catching him off guard as he watched her. He turned away, broke off a piece of bread and tossed it to a hopeful starling. 'Did she know him?' Rose persisted.

'No.'

'Not at all? They had never even spoken to each other?'

He saw her considering that, wondering how it would be to be married to a man you were given to as a prize. And he wondered how it would be to hold a woman he did not know, who had been given to him because their families had decided it would make a good match. She would have little say in the matter.

What would she think when she saw him? How

would she feel when he touched her? He'd never thought about it from a woman's viewpoint before.

'My mother told me once that he was the most beautiful man she had ever seen.' He'd had red hair too.

'Oh. She'd seen him, then?'

'Of course. He lived in the palace. The women were much more sheltered then, but there wasn't a thing they didn't know, or see. Ask Nadeem.'

'I will.'

'Is this for your article?'

Article? For a moment she'd forgotten about that. She'd write it because she'd promised him, but this wasn't anything to do with a magazine feature on a man who should have been Emir. She just wanted to know. She wanted to know everything about him. 'I'm filling in the background,' she said. 'Editors look for that kind of detail; the readers enjoy it.'

'I'll bet they do.'

'No... Not like that.' He continued to toss scraps of bread to the birds. 'Really. They are simply fascinated to see a life lived so differently from their own.' And it was different. On an intellectual level she'd always known that, but somehow on a personal one it hadn't seemed to matter. Apparently it did.

'Shouldn't you have a tape recorder? Or a notebook?'

'I usually do, but my bag was left behind when you issued your rather pressing invitation.' She shrugged. 'Don't worry, I'll send you a draft so that you can correct any errors. I wouldn't want to write anything that would embarrass her.'

He glanced back at her. 'Her?'

'Your mother.'

'Oh, yes. Maybe you would like to talk to her yourself? Nadeem will arrange it, if you like.'

'Does Nadeem do everything in your family?'

'My younger sister, Leila, is too busy raising her children, and my mother does charity work, has a busy social life.' He shrugged. 'Nadeem was always different. She demanded she be sent to school in England, went on to study medicine in the States.'

'And her father let her go?'

'Her mother—our mother—persuaded him. She'd been to Scotland with my father. He insisted and he was refused nothing... She'd seen a different life for women there.'

'One that she would have liked for herself?'

That he couldn't say. 'You'll have to ask her yourself. Of course Nadeem was warned by everyone that no man would want to marry her once she'd left the protection of her home.'

'I doubt she was entirely alone,' Rose remarked, somewhat drily.

He finally managed a smile. 'No. She had a positive entourage of protective females in tow. And her husband is a doctor, too, with more liberal ideas than most men. He even allows her to work.'

'Allows her to work? *Allows* her to work?' She tried to imagine her mother's reaction to such a display of chauvinism. 'Well, that *is* liberal.'

'He didn't have much choice. She refused to marry him until he agreed. She runs a women's clinic in town.' He smiled, a little grimly. 'It won't have been included in your tour of the highlights of Ras al Hajar; the needs of ordinary women never featured very high on Abdullah's list of priorities.' He tossed the remainder of his lunch to the birds. 'Tell me about your husband.'

'Michael?' She wanted to ask about Nadeem, the clinic, his own priorities, not talk about herself. 'Why?'

Because. He wanted to know. He knew he shouldn't ask, but he couldn't leave it. 'Just filling in the background,' he said, using her own words back at her. He was interested in the details, a life lived so differently from his own, where a wife was a partner, not a possession. 'We've got all afternoon. You can ask me a question and then it's my turn. That's fair, surely?' He took her silence for assent. 'He raised horses, you said.'

'I'm supposed to be interviewing you, Hassan.'

'Racehorses?'

There was a pause, then she nodded. 'Yes. Racehorses.' Then, 'Did she love him? Your mother?'

That was it? Two words? Maybe he should try it on her, let her see how much background she got that way. Except of course he couldn't. He didn't know what his mother had felt for his father. She had been his wife. That was enough. 'Love is a western emotion. A late-twentieth-century one at that.'

'You think so?'

'It's a fact.'

'Yet literature has always cherished lovers… Abelard and Heloise, Tristan and Isolde, Lancelot and Guinevere.'

'Romeo and Juliet,' he added. 'Maybe I should have said happy endings were a late-twentieth-century development.'

'I'll put that down as a ''don't know'', shall I?'

'Who ever knows about other people's lives?' He pulled a cushion towards him, tucked it beneath his elbow. She was near enough to touch, curled up on the rug totally unconscious of the soft curve of her breast within the compass of his hand. He was tormenting himself. He should move. But Rose Fenton wasn't that easy to shake off. He'd just have to try and keep his mind focused on higher things. 'Tell me about your husband,' he repeated, failing miserably.

'That's too general,' she protested. The coolly probing journalist, expecting him to bare his soul for her readers, was suddenly in full retreat as he turned the tables on her.

'You answered my last question with one word. This time you'll have to work a little harder, or my attention will begin to wander,' he warned. *As if.*

Rose poured herself a glass of iced tea from the flask. She glanced questioningly at Hassan, he nodded and she poured one for him as well. Putting off the moment. Working out what she would say as she turned the cold glass in her hands, pressed it against her hot cheek.

'I'd just come down from university. I was at a loose end until I started work in the autumn and Tim asked me to help him straighten out a truly terrible house he'd moved into. I went out on a call with him late one night to the stables and I met Michael.' She sipped the tea.

'And?'

She shrugged. 'Instant attraction.' And he hadn't been as difficult about it as Hassan. 'Of course my mother said I was just looking for a father figure.'

'I wondered if he was older than you.'

Rose pulled a face. 'His children were older than me.

Twenty-six and twenty-four, going on eight: a pair of
sulky brats more concerned about losing their inheri-
tance than whether Michael was happy.'

'Was he happy?' The question was unforgivable, in-
trusive. He knew it, but, despite the fact that his life
had always been cushioned by privilege, by wealth,
he'd found that simple happiness—that feeling on waking each morning that he was glad to be alive—had
tended to elude him in adult life.

'I hope so. I was. He was the dearest man, and I
must have complicated his life enormously.'

'With his children?'

'With his children, his ex-wife, his friends. None of
them approved. With the men it was just plain envy,
but their wives...' With their wives it had mostly been
panic. If Michael could do it, so could their men. 'He
must have known how it would be, but I threw myself
at him in the most disgraceful way.' She smiled as she
remembered. They were good memories, he could see,
and the knowledge cut him to the quick. Then the smile
faded. 'The sweet man didn't stand a chance.' Hassan
could believe it. 'He was far too much of a gentleman
to let me fall. So kind.'

'Kind.' Hassan repeated the word. He hoped the girl
Nadeem chose for him would be able to say as much.
But when he looked at Rose, choked back the feelings
that boiled up in him, he knew that kindness was not
enough. For a second their gazes locked, and he saw
that she had realised it too. 'Rose...' Her name was like
a match to a fuse, and as he moved to bridge the distance between them he knew that, fight it as he might,

the explosion had been inevitable since the moment he set eyes on her.

'No...' Rose felt as if the word had been torn from her throat. Desire to be held by him, loved by him, swept through her like a forest fire, and an hour ago she would have gone into his arms without a thought for sense or reason.

But not now. He was to be married. So what if it was to a woman he didn't know, didn't care about? It would still be meaningless, wrong, lust instead of love.

Even as he brushed back the scarf she'd draped so demurely about her head in a gesture that left her feeling utterly naked, even as he bent to press his lips to her breast and she burned for him, she knew that this time she must not give in to her own desperate desire.

'No, Hassan...' The painful words were wrenched from her, and she pushed away his hand as she staggered to her feet, chokingly hot. 'Let me go.' She clutched at her dress. How could she have forgotten to fasten it? Surely he would think it deliberate.

Maybe it was. He'd tried, heaven knew how he'd tried to keep his distance. But she had unbuttoned her dress, tormented him, and even then, when he'd stopped her, she'd sat beside him with it gaping open like the most appalling tease...

Burning with shame, she grabbed the edges and, screwing them together in one hand, she rushed to the stream, wading in until she was waist deep, only then releasing the dress to dip her hands into the water and throw it over face and neck, over her breasts and shoulders, until she was soaked.

It made no difference. And when she turned, she knew why. Hassan was right behind her.

She turned, eyes huge, her hair clinging in wet strands to her face, and Hassan felt the breath knocked from him. The thin silk clung to her, even where it was open to the waist it clung to her, moulding itself to her, defining her as a woman.

She was tall, lithe, stunningly beautiful. She was his equal. His perfect partner. Their sons would be strong, weaned on her courage. The daughters he longed for would mirror her beauty.

But to have them, to have her, he would have to leave his home, live in her world, watch her leave him to cover the latest fast-breaking story in some trouble spot, out of his sight, out of his protection. He could not do it.

He must not do it. He was needed here. But he groaned as he reached for her, gathered her to him and held her.

For a moment she resisted him, her eyes fierce. 'No, Hassan.' Her voice was husky with a need that matched the leaden weight in his loins, but it seemed that at last she, too, had recognised the necessity of fighting the attraction.

He made the kind of soft noises that would gentle a skittish horse. 'I hear you, Rose. It's all right. I understand. But come now. The water is too cold. You'll take a chill.'

Or maybe the water wasn't cold. It was simply the chill that had seized his heart. But she seemed incapable of movement, so he gathered her up, lifted her into his arms and carried her out of the water and along the rocky path to his quarters. The way was empty; his men had found excuses to take themselves out of sight, out of hearing.

Nothing could more plainly have shown that they approved his choice. The older men had been surrogate fathers to him, teaching him as they had taught their sons. And their sons were his boyhood friends.

They had seen in Rose the same qualities that he admired—courage, strength of purpose, an indomitable will—and they had shown their respect by referring to her as *sitti*, their lady, by their eagerness to please her.

For them it was so simple. He desired her, he would make her his own and she would never leave his house. His grandfather wouldn't have had a problem with that. If you want her, take her, he would have said. Take her and keep her. Give her children and she will be content.

Unable, unwilling to do that to her, he suspected that his own status would be severely dented.

Despite the heat steaming their soaking clothes, by the time they were inside Rose was shivering uncontrollably. He set her on her feet, found her a towel. She took it, held it. 'Rose, please, you need to get out of that dress,' he prompted, and turned away to search the dresser for the soft pashmina robe that had been his mother's wedding gift to his father and went with him everywhere. When he turned back she was trying desperately to finish what she had started with the buttons, but without success.

'I'm s-s-sorry,' she stammered, through chattering teeth. 'My hands are sh-shaking too much.'

'Hush, don't fret. I'll do it.'

'But—'

'I'll do it.' But the wet loops had tightened over the buttons and it was taking too long. In desperation, he took the edges of the silk, his fingers hot against the chill of her skin, and tore it free, so that it sank with its own soggy weight to the floor.

He'd arranged for the wife of one of his men to go into the new shopping mall to buy clothes, underwear for Rose. Confronted with her choice, he had to admit the woman had spent his money imaginatively.

As he unfastened the scrap of lace that cupped her breasts, eased the matching panties over her hips, he was grateful for his own plunge into the chill water of the stream, grateful for the cold wet cloth that clung to him, keeping the fuse on slow burn.

'Come,' he said, folding her into the comfort of the rich blue robe, feeding her arms into the wide sleeves, wrapping it about her, knowing that she would be warm in moments. He wanted to keep holding her. Instead he took the towel and rubbed at the wet ends of her hair. Then he threw back the covers and lifted her into bed. He would have given everything he had to join her there. Instead he pulled the comforter over her, tucked it around her. 'I'll get you something warm to drink.'

'Hassan...' He waited. 'I'm sorry. So sorry. I think about what I want and I just go for it. I did that to Michael. I needed him and it just didn't occur to me that he might not have needed me—'

He was at her side in a heartbeat. 'Hush...' he whispered, his fingers on her mouth. 'Don't say that. He was the luckiest of men. A man who could die with your name on his lips could regret nothing...' His eagerness to reassure her betrayed him. Even as he snatched back his traitorous fingers she reached out for him, held his hand against her face. 'Whose name will be on your lips, Hassan?'

He could not say. Must not. But it made no difference. She knew. 'You mustn't do it, Hassan.' He refused to help her, refused to ask the question, but she needed no assistance from him. 'You cannot marry some poor girl who will love you...'

'Rose!' Too late he tried to stop her, but she was relentless.

'Some girl who will love you, because she will not be able to help herself, Hassan. She will love you and bear your children and if you do not love her in return, you will break her heart.'

'Hearts do not break,' he lied. 'She will be content.'

'It isn't enough. Not for a lifetime.'

No. It would never be enough. But he retrieved his hand and made a determined effort to restore a semblance of sanity to a situation that was quickly spiralling out of control. 'You would have me spend my nights alone?' he enquired harshly.

'I would have you remember your honour.'

Honour? She was beginning to sound exactly like his sister, with her talk of blood or gold... And he remembered his own utterly idiotic agreement that marriage might be the only way to redeem himself. For a moment the siren call of temptation filled his head, a selfish longing strong enough to taste. But there was no honour to be had walking that slippery path. It was time to put an end to this.

'I remembered my honour, *sitti*,' he said coldly,

standing, determined to walk away, 'when you had quite abandoned yours.'

'Is that right?' She flushed angrily, pushed herself up onto her elbow. 'Well, I hate to disagree with *my lord*, but I'd have said we were about even on the day.'

And as anger heated her from the inside out, something clicked inside her brain. On the day. On this day. On this day they might consider themselves even, but Hassan was still deep in her debt. Nadeem had said so.

Gold, blood or honour. She had the right to choose.

Today she had used Hassan's standards to bring him back to her side. Could she use them to keep him there and put an end to this nonsense about an arranged marriage? She half believed he'd made it up simply to keep her at a distance. Except she knew he would not lie, which was why it had worked so well. Instead of seizing the moment, as she'd planned, she'd rushed into the water to cool herself off.

But just for a moment she believed…oh, it was crazy, but hadn't Nadeem said he would never be happy with a traditional bride? Hadn't she said to leave everything to her, she would arrange a marriage?

Marriage? She had to be crazy. She'd had too much sun. It was too soon to be thinking like that. Yet she'd known with Michael, from the moment he had looked up from his sick horse and anxiety had changed to a smile. She hadn't allowed petty-minded people or her mother's psychological dissection of their relationship to spoil their short time together.

And marriage had to be in Hassan's mind too, or why would he resist her so strenuously? He thought she was wedded to her career, travel, and had made the unilateral decision that she could never be happy with him. A selfish man would not have cared.

And the anger seeped away from her. 'Stay with me, Hassan,' she said, in a voice she scarcely recognised. And she lay back amongst the pillows. 'Stay with me.'

'Rose...please... I cannot.'

She was relentless. '*Sidi*, you must.'

'I need to change, my clothes are soaking...' he said, clutching at straws.

'Then you'd better take them off or you'll be the one with a chill.' She waited for a moment, and when he did not move, she said, 'Can you manage? Or do you need some help with the buttons?'

'It's not the buttons that are giving me trouble,' he said. 'It's you.' But he sat on the camel stool and tugged off his wet boots. Then he crossed to the chest and tugged at one of the drawers and began searching for something dry to wear.

Rose watched him for a moment, then she wriggled out of the soft pashmina gown. 'Try this,' she said.

Hassan turned and let slip one brief, desperate word as he saw the blue robe she was offering him, warm from her body. His mouth dried, his heart pounded, the heavy drag of his need for her became so intense that even to move would be torture. 'What do you want, Rose?'

'You keep asking me that, but you already know the answer.' She was lying back against the pillows, her damp curls tumbled about her face, her naked shoulders cream silk against the white linen, her throat begging to be framed in the lustre of pearls. 'You have to settle with me before you can even think of marriage, *sidi*. I'm calling in the debt.'

'The debt?' Could he pretend that he didn't understand? He could try, but she wouldn't be convinced.

'You said I could have whatever I wished.'

He felt bruised, beaten, as if he'd been fifteen rounds in the ring with a heavyweight. Round one had been in the plane, when she'd done something incredible with those eyes, shaking his faith in his invincibility. Then, in the back of the Land Rover she'd touched his face and he'd gone down briefly. As for last night—well, last night he'd kissed her and she'd nearly had him out for the count. He'd only just made it, and twice today she'd had him on his knees. He was on them now, and going down...

'I meant it. Name your price. Your heart's desire.'

'I want—'

Let it be diamonds. Or her weight in gold...

She let the robe drop, held out her hand to him, murmured his name like an imperceptible caress.

'Hassan.'

Almost nothing, the merest breath across the skin. The down feather from a duck would make more impression. And yet...and yet...the sound of his name filled his head, echoed there until his skin shivered with the impact of it. It called to something deep within him, all the longings, the need...

She'd looked into his soul, seen the emptiness, and the siren call of his name upon her lips promised that within her arms he need never be alone again.

Their fingertips touched, entwined, held fast.

CHAPTER NINE

HASSAN, his head propped upon his hand, lay on his side and watched the gentle rise and fall of her breast. Rose slept like a child, flat on her back, completely defenceless, as if certain that nothing in the world could hurt her.

There was a sweet artlessness in the pleasure she took in her own body, and from his, that suggested no one ever had, and he prayed that it would always be so.

Her lashes stirred against her cheek and she sighed, stretched, smiled at her dreams. For a man inured to the idea of love, the last few days had been a revelation, an awakening, and this was a moment to rend his heartstrings. Forcing himself away from her warmth, away from her love, he thought it was as well that heartstrings made no sound.

Everything had changed and yet nothing had changed. They were entirely different people and yet remained locked into their own cultures, their own expectations.

She would still leave, because her life, her real life, happened somewhere else. He would still remain in Ras al Hajar, because despite everything it was his home.

The memories they had made during the last few days and nights would have to be enough to last a lifetime, because there was no solution to their situation, only an inevitable heartache for an impossible dream.

Outside it was bright, clear, cold enough to fog his breath. Below him the oasis was still, the only sound that of the whickering of a restless animal in the stone corral.

'Hassan?'

He turned, reluctantly. Rose, tousled from sleep, wrapped in the blue robe, her hair kissed by starlight, was all a man could desire. 'I'm sorry, I hoped not to disturb you.'

'It's too late for sorry,' she said, laughing softly, 'you disturbed me the minute I set eyes on you.' Her eyes were liquid as she lifted her hand to his cheek, rubbing the backs of her fingers gently against the bone.

It was an invitation a man would have to be heartless to resist, and if he had learned anything in the blissful hours, days they had spent together, outside of the world, it was that he had a heart. All the hard work of putting some space between them was undone in that moment as he succumbed to temptation and was rewarded with the tug of her teeth against his lower lip, followed by the teasing caress of her tongue.

But maybe she could sense the distance he strived for, because after a moment she eased back, looked up into his face. 'You've found Faisal, haven't you?' she said.

Straight to the point, no messing. Already she could read him better than a book. She would be a hard woman to deceive. He'd tried it with his brave talk of an arranged wedding; she'd seen straight through him.

'Yes. He's on his way home.' He could not keep

himself from looking at her, seeing the effect on her at
his admission that their idyll was at an end.

Her hand rubbed softly at his sleeve in a gesture of
comfort. 'That must be such a relief for you.'

'Yes.' And no. He'd begun to suffer from the crazy
delusion that they could stay where they were for ever.
Crazy. Even if Faisal had remained on the loose, he
would have had to take Rose home. Her mother had
arrived with the news crew from her network and she
was not hanging around patiently while Abdullah
wrung his hands and said his men were doing everything possible. According to Nadeem, Ms Pam Fenton
was giving His Highness a seriously hard time. Having
come to know her daughter so well, he would have
expected nothing less.

'What about the girl he was with?' Rose asked.

'The girl?' He hadn't thought to ask, and Simon
Partridge, in a hurry, hadn't mentioned her. 'I'm sure
Partridge will make arrangements to ensure that she
gets home safely...' He paused, then added, 'With adequate compensation for her interrupted vacation.'

Rose suspected that this throw-away line was some
kind of attempt to provoke her, remind her that he
wasn't one of her 'English gentlemen'. She already
knew him too well to be deceived.

'Yes, I'm sure he will.' And she wondered what
compensation might be considered adequate for her
own interrupted holiday. Blood, gold or honour. Blood
would be unthinkable. Gold, insulting. There was no
contest, really. She stepped away from Hassan, stepped
from beneath the wide awning and into the darkness.

He reached out for her, his hand staying her. 'Where are you going?'

'Up there.' She pointed to the rise above the camp. 'Come with me. I want to stand up there with you and look at the sky.' She looked up at him, lifted his hand from her shoulder and kept it in hers. 'It seems so close out here in the desert, as if one might touch the stars.'

'You want to touch the stars?'

'The moon,' she said, taking in the thin silver sickle of the rising moon in a wide sweep of the heavens. 'The stars…'

'That's all? Why not a couple of planets while you're about it?'

'Why not?' She challenged his flippancy. 'With you to lift me I know I can do anything.'

His smile faded. 'There's something about you, Rose, that almost makes me believe you could.'

Just hold on to that thought, Hassan, she thought, as they walked together to the top of the high ground above the camp, where the heavens were a huge, star-filled dome above them. *Just hold on to that thought.*

Rose stopped as, away to the west, a meteorite streaked across the sky in a shower of falling stars.

'Look—look at that!' she whispered. 'It's so beautiful. Did you make a wish?'

His hand tightened imperceptibly over hers. 'Our destiny is written, Rose.' Then, glancing down at her, 'Did you?'

'I think it was my destiny to be standing here with you tonight at just the moment that star fell. It was my destiny to make a wish.' He waited, not asking, knowing that she would tell him. 'It was nothing dramatic,' she said, after a moment. 'Wishbones, wishing wells, falling stars—I always make the same one. That the people I love will be happy and safe.'

She thought he sighed at that. 'Nothing for yourself?'

He expected her to say that she wished to stay here always? Did he hope for it, just a little? 'That *was* for me. If they are happy and safe nothing else matters.' Then she smiled. 'Besides, the little things, like destiny, I can handle myself. I got myself here at just the right moment, didn't I?'

'You are so...so...' The words erupted from him. He wasn't exactly angry, Rose thought, he was simply at a loss to understand her head-on attitude to life, a determination to bend events to her will.

'So...what?' she asked. She really shouldn't tease him, she thought, he wasn't used to it. 'Assertive, perhaps?' She offered him the word, quite unable to resist the temptation. Getting no immediate agreement, she sighed dramatically. 'No, I thought not. You just think I'm wilful, don't you? Wilful and obdurate and bloody-minded—'

His fingers stopped her mouth. 'Resolute,' he countered softly. 'Uncompromising.' His hand strayed to a wayward curl and he tucked it behind her ear. 'Blessed with fire and spirit.'

'Same thing,' Rose said, a little huskily.

'Not quite.' Not at all. The one was infuriating, the other enchanting, and there was no doubt in his mind which of those words applied to Rose Fenton. She was enchanting, and he was undoubtedly bewitched because inside his head other words crowded forward, pushing their claim to be recognised. Words like…*unexpected, rare, lovely*…like a rose in the desert. And in that moment he knew which of all his possessions he would give her. An unspoken declaration of his love, something that, whenever she looked at it, touched it, would bring back this moment.

'Have you ever seen a desert rose?' he asked.

'A desert rose? Is it like a rock rose?' She glanced around, as if expecting to see one growing at her feet. 'My mother has a yellow one growing in a sink garden—'

'No, it's not a flower, not a plant of any kind. It's a crystal formation. Selenite.' *Unexpected, rare, lovely.* 'They're pink sometimes, and the crystals look like petals. You find them, if you know where to look, in the desert.'

'And?'

And what? His mind was playing games with him; he was too close to betraying his heart to this woman. 'And nothing, except the coincidence of your name. It just occurred to me that I found you in the desert, that's all.'

'Like a desert Rose.' He thought she might have smiled, but instead she just gave a little sigh. 'We'll have to leave tomorrow, go back into town, won't we? Back to the real world.'

Straight to the heart of the thing, his desert Rose. 'I wish things could be different, but we don't have a choice. We both knew that this couldn't last.'

He had decided it couldn't last; Rose preferred to make her own decisions. There were always choices, but it took a special kind of courage to cut through difficulties that appeared insurmountable, courage and trust and a belief that nothing could destroy you except your own self-doubt. Her mother had taught her that. Her mother hadn't wanted her to marry Michael, but she'd given her the strength to withstand the prejudice of petty-minded people who had tutted ominously over the age difference, declared it would all end in tears.

She could do it again.

She would give a little, he would give a little, and their small sacrifices would be rewarded a thousandfold. She knew that. Hassan, she suspected, was going to take some convincing.

Hassan was right about tomorrow, though. Nothing could stop real life intruding, but they still had what was left of the night, a few hours of magic before the world crowded in on them.

'Tomorrow will take care of itself, my love,' she said, lifting his hand to her lips, touching his cold knuckles to her cheek. Then she looked up into his face. 'Right now we should be making the most of the little time we have left.'

They had made the most of their time, the tenderness of their lovemaking bringing him almost to tears. But even though it would break his heart to leave her, he would end it here. This would always be their special place, and the memories they had made would remain untarnished by the inevitable slide into discord when their worlds clashed.

He left the tent early, and this time, exhausted, she did not stir, even when he brushed a strand of hair from her cheek. Kissed her softly. Whispered goodbye. Placed his small gift on the pillow beside her.

It was nothing precious. He would have showered her with precious jewels, anything her heart desired, but he knew she would be insulted, offended by such things. If he'd learned anything from Rose Fenton, it was that a gift from the heart was worth more than gold. And knowing that she had a part of him with her would be a comfort in the lonely years ahead.

Rose stirred, woke, and knew instantly that she was alone. That he had gone. She was not surprised. Last night he had been so tender, and when he had kissed her she had seen a shimmer of tears silvering the steely grey of his eyes. But he had still gone.

And people said *she* was obstinate.

What would it take to convince him? Maybe she should insist, make Tim demand that he marry her, then he'd have no choice. But the thought of Tim forced to confront Hassan with his duty just made her smile and this was serious.

Besides, he had to make the decision himself. She reached for his pillow, hoping to draw inspiration from its closeness. Instead her hand closed over something rough, hard. She knew instantly what it was. A desert rose. He'd left her a desert rose. And a note.

This is a part of me to take home with you, small return for the memories you leave behind.

Hassan.

She picked up the rose. It sat in her palm, small, exquisitely formed, but so different from the rosebuds that Abdullah had deluged her with. There was nothing soft about it, nothing to wither and die. It was fixed, immutable, unchanging.

Did he understand the message it conveyed? That this was an unconscious betrayal of his feelings? Rose thought not and she held onto the crystal for a long time, suddenly afraid that nothing she could do would ever move him to change his mind. Afraid that his will was like the rock and about as easy to soften. Afraid that he would make it impossible for her to get close enough to try.

'Miss Fenton?' The figure standing at the foot of her bed swam before her eyes. Tears? What use were tears? They never solved anything. 'Rose?' Rose blinked and a tall, slender woman, her dark hair streaked with silver, came into focus. 'Hassan asked me to come and take you home.'

'Home?' London, cold and bleak? No, this was home. Here with Hassan. 'I don't understand.' Then she did. He couldn't wait to get her out of the country...

'Your mother is waiting for you.'

Her mother? Then she realised who this was. 'You're Hassan's mother, aren't you? And Nadeem's. I can see the likeness.'

'Hassan said you wanted to talk to me.'

'It was kind of him to remember... I'm sorry, I don't know what to call you...'

The woman smiled, came closer, sat beside her on the bed. 'Aisha. My name is Aisha.'

'Aisha.' It didn't seem quite enough for this regal woman. 'Hassan must have more important things to worry about. And so must you, with Faisal coming home.'

'I've already spoken to Faisal… He called me from London. What have you there?'

Rose opened her hand for Aisha to see. 'It's a gift, from Hassan.'

'Well.' The older woman reached out, but stopped her fingers before they quite touched the rose. 'It's a long time since I've seen that.' She looked up, catching Rose unawares. Her eyes were dark, but they had the same powerful impact as Hassan's.

'He's had it a long time?'

'All his life.' Aisha's smile came not from her lips, but from somewhere deep inside. 'His father gave it to me, oh, so long ago. Before we were married, even—'

'Before?' Hassan's mother raised a finger to lips that curved in a smile that told its own story. It was a smile that knew all about love. 'And you gave it to Hassan…when you married your second husband.'

'I gave all of Alistair's things to Hassan. His clothes. This robe.' Her hand gently brushed against the soft blue pashmina gown that lay over the foot of the bed. 'All the things I had given him, all the things he had given me. One cannot take souvenirs from one love into another man's house. You have been married before, I am told, so you will understand.' Her words were softly inflected into something that was almost a question. Almost as if Aisha were testing her.

'Yes, I understand.' After she'd buried Michael she'd left his house and all that was in it for his squabbling family to pick over, taken off the rings he'd put on her finger and restarted her life from the point where she had left it on the day she had met him. She had married the man, not his possessions. Then she realised what Aisha had just said. 'How did you know that I'd been married?'

'Your mother told me when I had lunch with her yesterday. A most interesting woman—'

'She's here!'

'She arrived two days ago. Did you know that Hassan sent her a message? She did not know it was from him, of course, and I did not tell her. Just that someone had called to say that you were safe and well. He asked her not to tell anyone and she didn't.'

'My mother!' Rose made a move to get up, realised that she was naked and, blushing, stopped.

Aisha picked up the blue robe and held it for a moment, then handed it to her. 'Take your time, Rose. I'll walk for a while. It's too long since I was in the desert.'

The minute Aisha left, Rose scrambled from bed; she didn't have time to waste. Her mother was here? Her mother had heard from Hassan? Why hadn't he told her? Because he didn't want her know that he cared. The thoughts tumbled into her brain too quickly. She needed to think. She needed to slow down, take her time. Consider all the possibilities.

There had been a finality about the desert rose, the note. He had certainly meant them to be read as good-bye. She hadn't been able to convince the man. Could she convince the women in his life? His mother, his sisters. Would they help her?

She towelled her hair dry, then, unlike the Rose Fenton who would have grabbed the nearest pair of jeans and gone racing after the story, she sat at the mirror and carefully applied her make-up. Her *shalwar kameez* had been washed and returned to her and it lay neatly folded on the chest of drawers. She put it on and draped the long scarf over her hair.

By the time she was ready Aisha had returned from her walk and was relaxed upon the divan, drinking coffee. She turned, looked up at her and smiled. 'How charming you look, Rose. Would you like some coffee?'

'Coffee would be wonderful. And, if we have time, a little advice.'

As the plane taxied towards the airport terminal the Emiri standard was unfurled on the nose and fluttered its uncompromising statement. Hassan, standing second in line to greet the returning Emir, glanced at his cousin. Abdullah's jaw was set rigid, but in the face of the massed ranks of international newsmen he could do little other than wait to greet his youthful successor.

Behind him Hassan was conscious of Rose, standing out from the press of newsmen, not in the combat fatigues she usually wore in the dangerous places she reported from, but looking like a princess in silk and chiffon. Looking totally in control. Even the most hardened media men seemed to stand back slightly, give her space. One glance had been all that he permitted himself; one glance was all it had taken to know that it would never be enough.

The plane stopped, the steps were wheeled into place, the door swung open and Faisal appeared to a barrage of flashlights. Faisal, wearing jeans and a T-shirt that declared his support for his favourite American football team. Hassan was silently enraged. How could he? How could he take the moment so lightly? How could Simon Partridge allow this? They both knew how important this moment would be.

Then behind Faisal the slender figure of a young woman appeared. A California-girl blonde with a smile as wide as the Pacific. She was followed by Simon Partridge, his expression a mute plea for understanding.

Faisal loped, long-legged and agile, down the steps and crossed to Abdullah, bent over his hands in a gesture of respect. For a moment Abdullah looked triumphant. For a moment Hassan thought that he had thrown it all away. But then Faisal, with all the confidence of youth, extended his own hands and waited for Abdullah to return the honour, acknowledge him first as equal, then as lord.

For a moment Abdullah resisted, and Hassan held his breath, but Faisal did not move a muscle, simply waited, and after a moment that seemed to stretch time the Regent finally conceded to his King.

Faisal then coolly moved on to Hassan, extended his hands, this time with a wry smile, as if aware that he was in for a tongue-lashing. Hassan's bow disguised a stony expression, one that hid a considerable degree of respect. The boy had become a man. And even without the trappings of a prince to lend him dignity, he had forced Abdullah to back down.

Rose watched this performance from a little distance, reporting the characters in the drama as a voice-over to the pictures being beamed by satellite to her news network. She noted, without comment, that the young woman was whisked away into a waiting limousine while Faisal went through the motions of the ceremonial arrival.

Then, as he crossed to the car, Hassan at his side, she called out. 'Are you glad to be home, Your Highness?'

'Very glad, Miss Fenton.' He stopped, crossed to her microphone. Hassan, clearly torn between a desire to leave a safe distance between them and keeping his young protégé on a tight rein, finally followed him, but remained a clear six feet away from her, his gaze fixed somewhere above her head. 'Although as you can see my journey was at rather short notice, hence the somewhat casual attire. We have all been most concerned about you.' He made it sound as if her disappearance had provoked his sudden return.

'I'm sorry to have been such a nuisance.' She had explained away her disappearance as the result of a sudden relapse of her illness, conveniently remembering nothing until waking in the kindly nursing of some wandering tribesmen who spoke no English but who had finally arrived at a distant village with a telephone.

Her mother might look knowing, and Tim was giving a fair impression of a pressure cooker about to blow, but she hadn't wavered in the telling and no one was indiscreet enough to ask any awkward questions.

Faisal's smile was warm. 'I'm glad to see that you are none the worse for your recent adventure.'

'On the contrary. The desert is an awe-inspiring place, sir, and the hospitality of your people boundless.'

'Then we must ensure that you see more of both. Hassan will arrange a feast; we have much to celebrate.'

'I look forward to it.' But she didn't quite have the

nerve to meet Hassan's gaze. And she didn't ask about the pretty blonde. She didn't have to. She'd already had that story from Aisha.

Hassan watched Faisal's car drive away from the airport, then he headed towards his own waiting car. 'What in heaven's name were you thinking of, Partridge? I know I'm not in your good books, but did you have to do that to me?'

'I didn't—'

'Surely you could have found him a suit to wear? And as for bringing his girlfriend along for the ride. Eyes were popping faster than flashguns when she stepped out of the aircraft behind him. If she had to come surely you could have managed it with a little discretion—' He bit back the words. With the scent of his love on his skin he had no business lecturing anyone on discretion. 'Who is she?'

'Her name is Bonnie Hart. It seems that Faisal married her two weeks ago.'

'Married!'

'You...we...interrupted their honeymoon.'

'They were on their honeymoon? With the world to choose from, he picked a cabin in the Catskills?'

'The Adirondacks.'

'It doesn't matter where...'

'I rather got that impression. And they didn't go far because Bonnie has to be back in college next week.'

'College! Please, give me strength. What planet is Faisal on?'

'I'd say he has his feet very firmly on this one. She's a lovely girl, very bright. She's an agronomist—'

'I don't care what she is. Faisal had no business marrying her.' He was supposed to marry some girl who had been carefully chosen for him. Someone with all the right political connections, who would bring honour to his house. 'Please,' he begged, 'please, Simon, tell me that this is some kind of elaborate wind-up.'

'Why on earth would I do that to you?'

Because of Rose… Hassan dragged his hands over his face. 'No reason. I was just clutching at straws. What on earth are we going to do with her?'

'Give her a large patch of desert to play with?' he suggested. 'She's got some tremendous ideas. Apparently Faisal met her when he went to visit that hydroponics station you asked him to look at.'

'You mean this is all my fault?'

'No, sir. Faisal isn't a boy any more. He's a man. And he has some very firm ideas about what he wants. I suggested the jeans would not meet with your approval. He told me, very politely, to mind my own business.'

CHAPTER TEN

FAISAL and his bride had been taken to the fort and were both waiting for Hassan in his private drawing room. That alone broke all the rules of social etiquette, but Faisal was completely unfazed. 'Bonnie, this is my big brother, Hassan. He growls, but he doesn't bite. At least not unless seriously provoked.'

'Then, honey, you'd better get out the Band-Aid, because I'd say you've just done a gold medal job of provoking him.' Bonnie, showered and changed from her jeans into a pair of even more disreputable cut-offs, grinned amiably and offered him her hand. 'I'm Bonnie Hart. I'm sorry to confront you with a *fait accompli*, but Faisal said if I wanted him I'd better make up my mind fast, because once you got him home and tucked up in your palace it would be too late.'

Hassan knew when to accept that something was beyond mending and smiled graciously. 'My brother was teasing you. As Emir, as he well knows, he can do whatever he wishes. You are most welcome to Ras al Hajar, Your Highness.'

'Your Highness? Please! I'm an American. We had a revolution to put a stop to that kind of stuff—'

'Bonnie, sweetheart, why don't you take a nap while I catch up on things with Hassan? You'll want to look your best when company comes calling.'

171

'And it will come calling,' Hassan assured her. 'When Princess Aisha hears the news—'

'Aisha? We spoke on the phone from London,' Bonnie said, 'and I can't wait to meet her. And Nadeem and Leila. Gorgeous names.'

Was he the only one not in on this particular secret? Was he such a monster that his entire family had conspired to keep this from him? Did they think he wouldn't understand? Five days ago they might have been right. 'If you like their names so much, perhaps you'd like them to help you choose something as your own official name before you're introduced to your people.'

She glanced at Faisal. 'Er, I don't know about that—'

'Not now, honey. Hassan is busting his breeches to give me hell, but he can't do that with a lady present.'

She laughed. 'Sure. I know when I'm not wanted. Simon, why don't you show me around?'

'Would you mind, Simon?' Faisal asked.

'For heaven's sake, Faisal, she's your wife,' Hassan protested as their laughter echoed down the hall. 'She can't go running around with her legs on show to the world like that.'

'You think it'll give the old boys heart failure?'

'Not just the old ones.'

'Aren't they great, though? Tell me, Hassan, how were Miss Fenton's legs? You didn't waste much time getting them all covered up, I notice.'

Hassan gritted his teeth. 'Rose Fenton wears whatever she chooses, but she has a fine grasp of what is acceptable. And now I really have to insist that you change into something more suitable for the *majlis*. It will be crowded this evening.' Every man of substance in Ras al Hajar would be coming to give respect to their new ruler. No one would want to be seen as wavering.

'I want you to take the *majlis* in my place this evening, Hassan.'

'The hand-over is a dangerous time, Faisal. It's not a good idea to confuse people.'

'I'm not confusing anyone. You are going to take the *majlis* because I am going to make a television broadcast.'

'Are you? When did you arrange that?'

'During the lay-over in London. I spoke to Nadeem and she said she'd set up a network link with Miss Fenton.'

Hassan refused to acknowledge yet another mention of Rose Fenton, certain that it was nothing but a ploy to distract him. Actually, it was doing a fair job, but he persisted.

'I see. And what do you intend to say?'

'Maybe you'd like to give me some help with that. How do you see the country moving forward, Hassan? What would you like to change?'

Hassan was surprised. He'd scarcely dared to hope that Faisal would be so swift to grasp the reins. 'You really want to know?'

'Of course. I want to know what you all think. I know what Nadeem wants, and Bonnie has some great ideas, too. I want to tell the people, Hassan, I want the people to know that they have a Head of State who cares about them more than himself.'

'Actually, that's not a bad idea. Once they've seen

you on television no one will have any doubt about who's Emir.'

'That's my intention.'

And once that was settled, Hassan decided, he would get Nadeem to sort out the bare-legged revolutionary princess, put her right about palace etiquette. It was the least she could do, having kept Faisal's marriage from him. 'I did begin to wonder if you were having doubts about this, Faisal. You've stayed away longer than you should. It gave Abdullah ideas—'

'Why would I have any doubts, big brother?' Faisal grinned. 'Now I'm Emir I don't have to put up with you giving me a hard time about a thing. Not even my choice of wife.'

'Your wife is your problem. As for the rest, don't count on it.'

Hassan paced the palace audience room, running over the radical plans they had made, wondering whether it would cause outrage or rejoicing.

Nadeem and her husband had been full of ideas for improving medical services, particularly for women and children. Leila had been unexpectedly forthright on the subject of compulsory education for girls. A study to consider the development of hydroponic farming had been Bonnie's contribution. Well, there was no shortage of water from the mountains; it made sense, although what people would make of a princess who farmed on water was anyone's guess.

How he'd wished Rose could have been there. She had so much to offer... He checked himself. There was nothing to be gained from dwelling on something that could never be, and he picked up the remote and turned up the sound on the television.

Faisal was wearing traditional robes, yet he still managed to look like an American football player. In the last year he'd put on muscle, mental as well as physical. He'd become a man and Hassan was proud of him.

Faisal began as they had planned, by thanking his cousin Abdullah for his careful stewardship of the country. He then promised that he would always put the good of the country first. This was followed by his plans for Ras al Hajar, his strategy for making it into an outward-looking country in which women would play their full part.

'I have tonight,' he concluded, 'signed the statutes for a new government department so that there is no delay in setting these plans in motion. You will hear more about this in the coming days and weeks, but I will tell you now that this department will be run for women, by a woman.'

Hassan frowned. Statute? They'd discussed the idea of a department for women's affairs, but hadn't settled anything, let alone who would run it. This wasn't in the final draft of the address they had agreed.

He turned as Simon Partridge joined him. 'What is this?' he demanded. 'What's Faisal doing?'

Rose, standing to one side of the studio watching the subtitles as Faisal's words were translated into English, was approached by a royal messenger who handed her a thick envelope with the royal seal.

She continued to watch the monitor as she broke the

seal, pulled out the thick document. Then she glanced away to read the short letter that accompanied it.

Dear Miss Fenton,
My mother and sister both believe you will be a shining addition to our country. Hassan will need you. Please stay.

Faisal.

Gordon was standing beside her. 'What's that?' he whispered, when she opened the accompanying document.

She opened her mouth, then closed it and shook her head, tucking the letter and contract away as quickly as her shaking hands would let her. 'I'll tell you later. What's happening?'

'He's winding up. Are you ready for the close to London?'

'Many years ago, when he knew he was dying, my grandfather chose me as his successor.' Rose watched the words scrolling, then glanced at the envelope in her hand and had a flash of premonition.

'Oh...'

'What?'

She pressed her fingers to her mouth and shook her head.

'I knew, everyone knew, that I was not his first choice. Political necessity is, however, a hard task master.

'I have been Emir for one day, and in that day, with the help of my family, I have taken enormous pleasure in moving this country forward into a new era. I will continue to do that throughout my life, not as your Emir, however, but as his most faithful servant and subject…'

Hassan stared at his aide. 'You knew he was going to do this?'

'He swore me to silence.'

'You are my aide.'

'Yes, Excellency. But Faisal is Emir, or he is until midnight.'

'I won't let him do this, Simon.'

'Well, I'm sure Abdullah would be more than happy to resume his place, if you allow it.' Simon Partridge turned to the television as Faisal concluded his address.

'From midnight tonight I freely and gladly surrender all my claims to the throne of Ras al Hajar and pass that heavy burden to my grandfather's rightful heir and successor, his first grandson, my brother, Hassan.

'At the summit there is only room for one. It is a lonely place, and it gives me much pleasure to tell you that my last act as Emir will be to sign a contract of marriage for Prince Hassan. I wish every happiness to him and his chosen princess, along with my vow and pledge to support and honour him as Emir of Ras al Hajar.'

He was trapped. The *majlis* was mobbed. Apparently there wasn't a man in the country who didn't want to make his obeisance to his new lord.

Faisal had been so clever. Arriving in jeans and T-shirt and trailing a foreign wife. Even the waverers were glad to cleave to the tradition that Hassan had always honoured.

What would they do if they knew that while he was sitting there, acknowledging his friends and his enemies alike, forcing himself to put names to dimly remembered faces, he was acknowledging that his young brother had more courage in his little finger than he had shown? That all he wanted to do was find Rose and tell her...tell her...that he loved her and beg her to stay.

It was after one o'clock before it was over, but he headed straight for the phone. 'Tim Fenton.' The voice sounded heavy with sleep. 'Is it the foal?'

'No. It's Hassan. I have to speak to Rose. Now.'

'Well, you can't.' Fenton sounded thoroughly smug about that. 'She's not here.'

'Where is she? She can't have left already—'

'I don't think her whereabouts is any of your business, Your Highness. And by the way, I resign.' He hung up.

An hour earlier his fortress had been thronged with people; suddenly it was empty but for servants, guards. Faisal had taken Bonnie to stay with Aisha before the broadcast. Now he understood why.

Nadeem...well, he'd told his sister to arrange a wedding and waste no time doing it. No doubt tomorrow she would make a formal call to tell him who she had chosen as his bride, inform him of the settlements, the wedding arrangements. Tomorrow would be soon enough. He was in no particular hurry to find out.

Rose spent a day with the kind of pampering she had only ever dreamed of. A top-to-toe grooming, a massage with essential oils, her hands painted with exquisite arabesques, first in orange henna, then in black, which Nadeem told her lasted much longer.

Pam Fenton was in her element too, watching, taking notes. 'Darling, you really are the most wonderful daughter. An absolute inspiration. First you marry a man old enough to be your father and give me enough material for a book. Now this.'

Rose, watching the progress of the delicate hand painting, didn't even turn her head. 'What is it about *this* that particularly pleases you?'

'Modern woman with a have-it-all career gives it all up to live in a harem.'

'Write a book that portrays me like that and I'll sue you.'

'Really? That'll be so good for sales.'

'It's not true, Mother. Nadeem lives a full and active professional life, as you well know. And I am going to be running a new government department set up to improve the lot of women; Abdullah never did anything for them. Why don't you stick around and study that? Help out, even?'

'Oh, please, darling. You don't even speak the language. And you'll be knee-deep in babies before you're much older.'

'I already speak French, German and Spanish, and my Arabic is coming along in leaps and bounds.'

'And babies?'

'They never slowed you down.'

'That's true. Actually, that would make an even better book...'

* * *

'*Rose Fenton!* Rose Fenton is going to run the new government department?' Hassan's heart was threatening to explode.

'Can you think of anyone more suitable?' Not in a million years. But that wasn't the point; surely the boy could see that? When he didn't immediately answer, Faisal shrugged. 'Of course you can't. She's the perfect choice, Hassan. She understands the media, knows how to communicate with people. I'm amazed at how quickly she's picking up the language.' He hesitated. 'Well, maybe not that amazed. When you have one-to-one tuition... You think it will be awkward for you, is that it?'

Awkward? What rubbish was the boy talking? He loved her. To see her, know she was near, that he could never touch her, never hold her. Awkward he could handle. This wasn't awkward; this was his worst nightmare.

'How long is her contract?'

'A year. I thought she would need that long to get the department up and running, sort out the priorities. After that, well, maybe she won't want to stay. Unless you can think of some way to persuade her?'

'Faisal—'

'Yes, Your Highness?' His innocent tone cut no ice with Hassan.

'I think perhaps you'd better go. Take your pretty wife and disappear for a year or two. By then I might have got over this compelling desire I have to wring your neck.'

'I give you a crown, a bride and a media queen all

in one day and this is all the thanks I get,' he retorted in disgust. 'Some people are impossible to please.'

'Go!'

Faisal raised his hands in surrender. 'I'm out of here,' he said, backing to the door. 'I'll, um, see you at the wedding.'

Hassan rose to his feet. 'There will be no wedding…' The words erupted from somewhere deep within him. 'There will be no wedding.' Whatever it took, he would stop it. If he could not have Rose, he would have no one. No one.

Nadeem stood back and smiled. 'Stunning. You look absolutely stunning. Don't you think so, Pam?'

'I wouldn't know. I can't see her.'

'Well, it wouldn't be right for Hassan to see her before they're betrothed. The clothing and jewels are enough to indicate that the girl beneath them is a suitable bride for an Emir.' She turned away as she heard a movement beyond the hangings that divided the room. 'He's arrived,' she whispered. 'Quickly, slip out this way, Pam.'

Hassan waited impatiently for his sister. He'd come to put a stop to this nonsense, whatever it cost. How on earth could the pair of them have plotted and planned and then landed him in a situation where to reject the bride they had chosen would cause more offence and bad feeling—?

'Nadeem.' He turned and crossed swiftly to his sister as she slipped through the heavy drapes.

'Hassan.' She took his hands. 'I'm glad to see you so eager. We're ready for you.'

'No. I'm sorry, but I came to tell you that I can't do this. There is no way I can go through with this marriage.'

'I don't understand. You asked me to arrange it without delay.' She looked deeply shocked. 'The contracts are signed.'

'Faisal overstepped himself.'

'He was thinking of you, Hassan. During this last week we have all been thinking of you.'

'I know.' He could not look her in the face. 'I know. This is my mistake, and mine alone, but I have a prior call on my honour. One that can never be expunged other than by marriage.'

'Rose?' she asked. 'You mean Rose?'

'Of course I mean Rose. Who else could there be?'

'But you assured me that you would deal with that—'

'I thought I could. I thought I had. I was mistaken.'

'Hassan, I have seen enough of Rose to be sure she would not bind you in any way that was disagreeable to you. Would you like me to speak to her?'

'*No.*' Then, more gently, 'No. It would make no difference. Whatever her answer, I will never be free. You see, I find that I cannot live without her.'

'You are in love with her, then?'

'She is...' He clenched his fist, laid it against his heart. 'Inside of me.'

Nadeem's smile was gentle as she took his hand and held it between hers. 'I understand, Hassan. And so will the girl who is waiting for you. You must explain your feelings, open your heart—'

'Nadeem, please—'

'She will understand; I promise you.'

'But—'

'Trust me.' Then, with the sweetest of smiles, 'I'm a doctor.' And, still holding his hand, she drew back the curtain for him. Behind it, in the centre of the room, stood a tall, slender young woman in a floor-length gown of vivid red silk thickly embroidered in gold thread. About her waist was a belt made from heavy gold mesh. Over her head was a veil so dense that he could see nothing of her features, or her expression.

He realised, too late, that he did not even know her name, and he half turned, but behind him the curtain had closed.

From beneath the veil, Rose watched him. She had not been happy about Nadeem's plan. There was no way she could marry Hassan without him knowing who she was. There was no way she would marry a man who would contemplate such a match.

But she need not have worried. Nadeem understood her brother better than he understood himself. She had known that he could never go through with such a marriage. And now he stood before her with instructions to open his heart, confess his love for another woman.

But his pain was heart-rending. She could put him through no more of it. She had heard enough, and she extended her hand to him. *'Sidi,'* she said softly.

Her hands were painted; she was dressed as his bride. How could he possibly begin to explain…?

'Lord,' she said again, in English, and something jarred deep inside him.

He took a step towards her. 'Who are you?'

'You know me, lord.'

'Rose…' He couldn't believe, didn't believe it. But her hand came into his like a sweet memory. 'You once said that if a man was fortunate enough to have you, you would make it your life's work to ensure that he wanted no other—'

'I meant it.'

'It didn't take a lifetime…' He lifted the veil. 'I love you. You are my life. Stay with me, Rose. Always. Live with me, bear my children, be my wife and my princess.'

Had he changed? Could he change? 'You want me to stay at home and raise your sons, Hassan?'

His hands went for her waist and he pulled her closer, his expression deadly serious. 'That sounds good to me.' She stiffened in his arms, but he was learning to tease a little. 'Do you think you could fit that in with your busy new career running a new government department?'

'You know about that?'

'Faisal confessed what he'd done about half an hour ago.'

'And you wouldn't mind?'

He minded. He didn't want her out of his sight for a minute. But if that was the price of keeping her, he would learn to live with it. 'You've got a contract signed by the Emir of Ras al Hajar. Who am I to argue with that?'

'And if I have to travel abroad, go to conferences—?'

'I'll hate it,' he admitted. 'But I love you, Rose…

I'll have you or no one. On any terms. The question is, my love, will you have me?'

'You have a contract signed by the Emir of Ras al Hajar,' Rose replied, lifting her hand to his face, touching her lips to his. 'Our destiny is written, Hassan, and who am I to argue with destiny?'

Coming this September from

AMERICAN ✦ ROMANCE®

You met the citizens of Cactus, Texas, in
4 Tots for 4 Texans when some matchmaking
friends decided they needed to get
the local boys hitched!

And the fun continues in

BY
JUDY CHRISTENBERRY

Don't miss...
THE $10,000,000 TEXAS WEDDING
September 2000
HAR #842

In order to claim his $10,000,000 inheritance,
Gabe Dawson had to find a groom for Katherine Peters
or else walk her down the aisle himself. But when he
tried to find the perfect man for the job, the list of
candidates narrowed down to one man—*him!*

Available at your favorite retail outlet.

Makes any time special ™

Favorite Harlequin Romance® author

Jessica Steele

brings you

THE
MARRIAGE PLEDGE

*For three cousins it has to be marriage—
pure and simple!*

Yancie, Fennia and Astra are cousins
who've grown up together and shared the
same experiences. For all of them, one thing
is certain: they'll never be like their mothers,
having serial meaningless affairs.
It has to be marriage—or nothing!

But things are about to change when three
eligible bachelors walk into their lives....

Titles in this series are:

THE FEISTY FIANCÉE (#3588) in January 2000
BACHELOR IN NEED (#3615) in August 2000
MARRIAGE IN MIND (#3627) in November 2000

*Available in January, August and November wherever
Harlequin Books are sold.*

HARLEQUIN®
Makes any time special.™

**Don't miss
an exciting opportunity
to save on the purchase of
Harlequin and Silhouette books!**

Buy any two Harlequin or
Silhouette books and save
$10.00 off future Harlequin
and Silhouette purchases

OR

buy any three
Harlequin or Silhouette books
and save **$20.00 off** future
Harlequin and Silhouette purchases.

*Watch for details
coming in October 2000!*

PHQ400

HARLEQUIN
Duets™